Twisted Christmas
The Next Generation

Twisted Christmas
The Next Generation

BY

TRACY WILSON

http://beautifulpublications.com

Published by
Beautiful Publications LLC
Stratford, CT 06614

PRINT ISBN: 978-1-7343352-0-0
EBOOK ISBN: 978-1-7343352-1-7

Printed in the United States of America

Dedication

This last book in the Twisted Series is dedicated to my nieces & nephews. Some of you are still young, and some of you are adults with children of your own. You'll see yourselves, you'll see your children, you'll laugh, and you'll love. Aunt Tracy is proud of you.

Chapter ONE

"Bazil..."

"Huh?"

"Bazil... wake up..."

"What's wrong? You want some more dick?" Bazil asked as he rubbed his eyes...

"Always – but that's not why I woke you up..."

"Is Jay alright?"

"Jay's fine... but we need to wake him up..."

"We do?"

"My water broke..."

"Oh shit – okay – I'm up!" Bazil said as he jumped up outta bed... "What should I do?"

"I'll get up and get dressed – you wake Jay up and get him dressed..." Beautiee said as she got up outta bed...

"Oh boy – Jay's not gonna like this..." Bazil said as he went to wake up Jay... "Jay... c'mon... wake up son..."

"I night night..."

"I know son – I'm sorry – we need to get ready – Mommy needs to go to the hospital..." Bazil said as he picked Jay up, got a fresh pamper, and some clothes..."

"Mommy sick?"

"No Jay – Mommy's having a baby..." Bazil answered as he changed Jay's pamper...

"My brother?"

"Yes Jay..." Bazil answered as he dressed Jay...

"Yaaaaaa!" Jay said as he clapped his hands...

"Troy – get up..."

"What's wrong?"

"My water broke..."

"When?"

"I'on know!"

"Why didn't you wake me up when it broke?" Troy asked as he jumped up outta bed...

"You said you was tired – I was tryin' to be nice – damn!"

"C'mere Keisha..." Troy said as he pulled her into a hug and held her..."

"I'ma kick your ass Troy..."

"I know... it's okay..." he said as he held her even tighter...

"I'm serious – this shit hurts..."

"Damn Keisha – you having contractions already?"

"Yea..."

"Oh shit – c'mon – let's get dressed – we need to get to the hospital..."

"I'm already dressed..."

"Oh shit – I ain't even see that – le'me hurry up..." he said as he got dressed in a hurry...

"Chandler..."

"Yes Starr?" Chandler answered as he rubbed his eyes...

"My water broke..."

"Oh shit – you're in labor?" Chandler asked as he jumped up outta bed...

"Yea..." Starr answered as she rubbed her stomach...

"Okay – I'll get dressed – then I'll help you get dressed..."

"I can dress myself Chandler..."

"I know – I just wanna make sure you're okay..."

"Oh God – Chandler!" Starr moaned as another contraction hit...

"Here – take my hand..." Chandler said...

"Chandler – it hurts!"

"I know – squeeze my hand…" Starr squeezed his hand as hard as she could until the contraction passed…

"I'm sorry…"

"What'd I tell you about apologizing?"

"I'm sorry…" she said as she started crying…

"Starr…" he said as he kissed her eyes, her tears, and her mouth… "you're having our girls – I love you…" he said as he kissed her…

"I love you too…"

"C'mon – let's get dressed…" he said as he helped her out of her pajamas…

"Okay…" she said as she sat still and let Chandler dress her…

"Okay – I'ma hurry up and get dressed – then we're going to the hospital…

"Theresa…"

"Yes Charles?" she answered sleepily…

"You wet the bed…"

"I did?"

"I think your water broke…"

"Oh my God!" she said as she sat up and looked down between her legs…

"You okay?"

"I'm a little wet…" she laughed… "But otherwise, I'm okay… oh God…"

"I'm here…" Charles said as he sat down on the bed beside Theresa and rubbed her back…

"We're having… a… baby!" she panted…

"Yes we are..." Charles said as he kissed her...

"Le'me hurry up and get dressed so we can get outta here before another contraction hits..." she said as she got up outta bed and took her nightgown off... "Charles – why are you standing there looking at me like that?" she snapped...

"You're so beautiful..." Charles said as he went over to her, pulled her to him, and kissed her...

"I love you Charles..."

"I love you too – let's get dressed..." he said as he started getting dressed...

"Okay..."

"Wayne..."

"Yes Mary?" Wayne answered sleepily...

"I'm in labor..."

"Wait – what?" Wayne asked as he sat up in the bed...

"I'm in labor..." she repeated...

"Okay – I'll get dressed..." he said as he got up outta bed...

"Oh God – here comes another one..." Mary grunted...

"What can I do?"

"Rub my back..."

"Here?" Wayne asked as he started massaging her shoulders...

"Wayne!"

"Am I doing something wrong?"

"The contractions don't come up there..." she laughed...

"Oh – sorry..." he said as he rubbed her lower back...

"Oh God..." Mary panted...

"I'm right here..." Wayne said as he continued rubbing her back...

"Wayne..."

"Yes Mary?"

"Stop touching me..."

"You sure?"

"I don't know – just stop..."

"Okay – I'll get dressed..."

"I'm sorry..."

"I know..." Wayne said as he bent down and kissed her...

"I love you Daddy..."

"I love you too Mommy..."

Chapter TWO

"Welcome to Milford Hospital – what's your emergency?" the receptionist asked...

"My wife's in labor..." Bazil answered...

"And who's this little guy?" she asked as she came from behind the desk and bent down to look closer at Jay...

"Jay..." he answered...

"Hello Jay – I'm gonna take Mommy for a little bit – is that okay?"

"No!"

"Jay – I'll be right back – sit here with Daddy – okay?"

"Okay Mommy..." he answered as Beautiee went with the receptionist... "This is our triage nurse – she's going to take your temperature, your blood pressure, check your oxygen, and then we'll get you upstairs to maternity – okay?"

"Okay..." Beautiee said as she sat in the chair and the triage nurse checked her pulse and then proceeded to take her blood pressure... "Hello..." Beautiee said...

"I need to put this under your tongue..."

"Hello..." Beautiee repeated...

"Hi..." the triage nurse sighed...

"Long day huh?"

"Yea..." Beautiee put the thermometer under her tongue, waited for the beep, and gave the thermometer to the triage nurse...

"You're good – I just need to check your oxygen and then I need you to get in the wheelchair..."

"Okay..." Beautiee said as the triage nurse checked her oxygen and then opened the wheel chair for her to sit in... "Do I need to go back and register?"

"I'm sure your husband took care of that..." she laughed...

"Is that right?"

"Yea... it is..." she laughed...

"I made you laugh?" Beautiee asked...

"Don't mind me – it's just..."

"What?"

"I know who you are... and I know your husband too..."

"Okay... and?"

"I have all your books..."

"You do?"

"Yea – are you writing any more?"

"As a matter-of-fact... I'm writing my story..."

"Oh my God! I can't wait!"

"Really?"

"Yes Hunty!"

"Thank you..."

"You're welcome – and thank you!"

"You're welcome..."

"Could you do me a favor?"

"Sure..."

'I'm not supposed to do this – but can I take a selfie with you?"

"Of course..."

"Oh my God – thanks!" she squealed as she hurried up and took out her phone...

"Is she done yet?" the receptionist asked as she came in...

"Just about..." the triage nurse answered...

"Good – her son is looking for her..." the receptionist laughed as she left...

"Make sure you tag me in that picture when you post it..." Beautiee said as the triage nurse pushed her back out to the waiting area...

"Oh I will – don't worry..." she laughed...

"Are you ready to have our son?" Bazil asked when he saw Beautiee...

"No! Mommy's having my brother!" Jay said...

"Yes Jay – Mommy's having your brother..." she laughed as she took Jay and Bazil pushed her towards the elevator...

"Beautiee!"

"Keisha?"

"Yea – wait for me!"

"You wanna wait for Keisha?" Bazil asked...

"Yea..."

"Okay..." Bazil sighed as he went back over to the waiting area...

"Mrs. Osgood – I thought you were going upstairs?" the receptionist asked...

"I was – I'm waiting for my best friend..."

"Oh wow – you're both having a baby – that's nice!" she beamed...

"Yea, yea, yea – it's nice – but this shit hurt!" Keisha snapped...

"I'm sorry Keisha..." Troy said...

"The fuck you keep saying you sorry for – that shit don't help with the contractions!" Keisha snapped. Troy just shook his head...

"C'mon Keisha – let's get you into triage – then you can go upstairs..." the receptionist said as she took Keisha to triage...

"Don't take it personal..." Bazil said as he patted Troy on the shoulder...

"I'm not – I just wish I could help her..."

"I wish you could too..." Beautiee agreed...

"Mr. Cochran – let's get her registered while she's in triage – then you can all go up together..." the receptionist said...

"Okay – here's our insurance..." Troy said as he handed her the insurance card...

"You'll be alright..." Beautiee said...

"I'll be alright – but will Keisha be alright?" he laughed... "She already threatened to kick my ass!"

"She'll be fine – the first one is always hard..." Beautiee said...

"Was it hard for you?"

"Well... it was crazy!" Beautiee laughed...

"What happened?"

"Mary helped us deliver Jay..." Beautiee laughed...

"Mary was at the hospital?"

"At the wedding..." Bazil answered...

"Wait – you had Jay – at Chandler's wedding?"

"On their wedding night..." Bazil answered...

"Oh wow – I gotta hear this..."

"Oh God – Bazil..."

"You havin' another contraction?"

"Yeeessss..." Beautiee grunted...

"Beautiee – you alright?" Keisha asked...

"Yea..." she grunted... "I'm just having... a... contraction!"

"Let's get them upstairs..." Bazil said...

"Okay Keisha – I gotchu..." Troy said...

"It's okay Mommy..." Jay said as he hugged Beautiee and they all went to the elevator...

"You ready?" Chandler asked...

"Yes... I'm ready... Uggh!" Starr answered...

"You okay Starr?" Theresa asked as she got to the elevator...

"Just... having... a... Uggh!"

"C'mon Starr – hold my hand – squeeze if you need to..."

"Okay..." Starr panted...

"Chandler – we need to get these ladies to the hospital!" Charles snapped...

"Charles – I'ma need you to calm down..." Chandler said as they all got in the elevator...

"I'm sorry – I didn't mean to snap – I'm just nervous..." Charles laughed...

"You think I'm not?"

"You're doing better than I am..." Charles laughed...

"Oh shit – here comes another one..." Theresa grunted as she squeezed Starr's hand...

"We're almost there – can you make it to the car?"

"I can... Uggh!" Theresa grunted...

"C'mon baby..." Charles said as he put his arm around Theresa and led her out the lobby to the car...

"Chandler... wait..."

"I'm right here..." Chandler said as he held Starr...

"Uggh!" she grunted as she grabbed Chandler's arm...

"You good?"

"I think so..."

"C'mon... I gotchu..." he said as he led her out the lobby to the car...

"Welcome to Mt. Saint Vincent – what's your emergency?" the receptionist asked as they all walked up to the desk...

"They're in labor..." Charles answered...

"Both of them?"

"Yea..." Chandler answered...

"Okay – who's going first?"

"You go!" Starr and Theresa said in unison as they bust out laughing...

"Okay..." the receptionist laughed... "But I can only take one at a time..."

"Can't we both go?" Starr asked...

"You want your friend to go with you?"

"Yea... Uggh!" she grunted...

"Let me tell the nurse..." she said as she went to triage... "Hey Candice..."

"Hey Connie – who's next?"

"We have two..."

"Okay – send me one of them..."

"She wants her friend to come with her..."

"That's fine..."

"Okay – I'll tell her..." Connie said as she went back out to the waiting area... "Okay ladies - Candice said - you can both go in..."

"Thank you..." Theresa grunted as another contraction came...

"C'mon ladies!" Candice said as she escorted them into the triage room...

"Okay – let's get your wives registered so we can get you upstairs to maternity..." Connie said...

"Okay – whatcha need?" Charles asked...

"I just need your insurance cards – I can get everything from there..." Connie answered...

"Okay Starr – I'm Candice – I'm the triage nurse here at Mt. Saint Vincent – I'm gonna check your blood pressure, your oxygen, and take your temperature – and then you'll go upstairs to have your baby..." she said as she proceeded...

"I'm having twins – girls..."

"Oh wow – that's nice – have you picked out any names?"

"Not yet..."

"Hmmm... your pulse is a little fast..."

"I'm nervous..."

"I know – but you need to relax – it'll be better for your babies – here – put this under your tongue..." she said as she handed Starr the thermometer and Starr put it under her tongue. Candice waited for the beep, took the thermometer out of Starr's mouth, and looked at it... "Everything looks okay – try to relax – if you can..."

"I'll... try..." Starr grunted as another contraction came...

"Okay – how are you feeling Theresa?" Candice asked as Theresa sat in the chair...

"I'm nervous too..."

"I understand – it's normal – especially when it's your first..." Candice said as she proceeded...

"This isn't my first..."

"Oh – I'm sorry – how old is your first?"

"I had a miscarriage..."

"I'm sorry – let's talk about this baby – do you know what you're having?"

"No – we wanted it to be a surprise..."

"That's the way it used to be – now everybody's doing gender reveal parties..."

"Yea – we didn't want a gender reveal party..."

"Okay – I need to take your temperature..."

"Okay... oh God..." Theresa panted...

"Squeeze my hand..." Starr said as she took Theresa's hand...

"Open..." Candice said. Theresa opened her mouth and Candice put the thermometer under her tongue. Theresa loosened her grip but continued to hold Starr's hand until the thermometer beeped and Candice took it out of her mouth...

"Okay – you ladies can go upstairs – wait here – I need to get another wheelchair..." she said as she got up and went to get a wheelchair from the waiting area...

"How's my wife?" Charles asked when he saw Candice...

"She's fine – I need to get this wheelchair so she can go upstairs..."

"You need help?"

"Sure – c'mon..." Candice answered as Charles and Chandler got up and followed Candice to triage...

"Chandler..."

"I'm here..."

"I'm ready..." Starr beamed...

"I'm ready too!" Theresa beamed...

"C'mon ladies – let's get you into these wheelchairs so you can go deliver your babies..." Candice said as she opened them up and they sat in them...

"You ready Chandler?" Charles asked...

"Hell yea I'm ready!" Chandler answered as they pushed Starr and Theresa to the elevator...

"Welcome to Michael Garron Hospital – what's your emergency?" the receptionist asked...

"My wife's in labor..." Wayne answered...

"Okay – I'll take you to see the triage nurse and I'll get the information I need to register you – okay?"

"Okay…" Mary panted…

"You okay Mary?" Wayne asked…

"I'll be alright…"

"You can go with your wife if you want – I just need your insurance information…" the receptionist said…

"Wayne – I won't be long…" Mary said as the receptionist escorted her to see the triage nurse…

"Okay – give me your insurance card – I'll register her – then you can go be with your wife…" she said…

"Here ya go…" Wayne said as he handed the receptionist his insurance information…

"Hmmm – how many pregnancies has your wife had?" the receptionist asked…

"Two…"

"Oh – so this is her third pregnancy?"

"No – this is her second – why do you ask?"

"She was seen at Planned Parenthood…"

"How do you know that?"

"Planned Parenthood is part of the hospital…"

"It is?"

"Sort of – all the OB'GYN doctors here do rotations at Planned Parenthood so your wife was added to the patient roster…

"I see…"

"Okay – here – you can go be with your wife now…" she said as she handed Wayne the insurance card…

"Thank you..." Wayne said as he took the card and then walked over to triage...

"Everything's fine – your wife is ready to go upstairs to maternity..." the triage nurse said as Wayne walked in...

"Let's go have a baby Mommy..." Wayne said as he pushed her out the room...

"Okay Daddy..." Mary said on her way out...

"Aww... God bless them..." the triage nurse said out loud.

Chapter

THREE

"Bazil... Uggghh!"

"Do I need to get the doctor?"

"Yes!"

"Okay – Here Jay – go to uncle Troy – Daddy'll be right back..." Bazil said as he handed Jay to Troy and then ran out the room and down the corridor...

"Mr. Osgood – what's wrong?" Kay asked...

"Beautiee said I need to come get you – c'mon!" Bazil said as he grabbed Kay by the hand and pulled her down the corridor to the room...

"Uggghh!"

"Waaaah! My brother hurt Mommy!" Jay cried...

"I'm here Beautiee – let's take a look..." Kay said as she looked under the sheet... "It's time for you to push – let me check on Keisha too while I'm here..."

"I'm aiight – take... Beautiee... Ugghh!"

"Le'me see how you're doing..." she said as she looked up under the sheet... "Hmmm – I don't see the head – I need to do a quick exam..."

"Now? Really?"

"Keisha – I need to see if you've dilated..."

"Whatever – just hurry the fuck up!"

"I'ma let you have that one..." she laughed as she examined Keisha... "Your wife's starting to dilate – it will be time for her to push soon – c'mon Bazil – your son will be here any minute..." she said as she started to roll the bed down to the maternity room...

"No! I want Mommy!" Jay cried...

"Beautiee..." Kay started to say but Beautiee interrupted her...

"Give him here..."

"Beautiee – you can't..."

"Bazil..." Beautiee panted...

"Stay here with Uncle Troy..." Bazil said as he gave Jay to Troy and then followed behind Kay to the delivery room...

"Oh God – he's coming!" Beautiee yelled. The assistants got her legs up in the stirrups just in time...

"Beautiee – push!" Kay yelled as Bazil got the hospital gown on, got his phone out, and started recording...

"Uggghh!"

"Beautiee – I can see him!" Bazil said as he started to cry...

"One more push Beautiee – c'mon!" Kay yelled...

"Uuuggghhhh!"

"He's here!" Bazil cried...

"You wanna cut the cord Daddy? I'll hold the phone..." Kay said...

"Okay..." Bazil said as Kay gave him the scissors and he cut the cord. Bazil picked up his son and cried... "Hello Joseph... I'm your Daddy... and this is your Mommy..." he said as he brought Joseph up to Beautiee so she could see him...

"Hi Joseph..." she said...

"We did it..." Bazil said as he kissed her...

"Okay – I need you to take your phone – we need to clean Joseph up so you can take him to meet his brother – then we need to get Keisha in here..." Kay said...

"Okay..." Bazil said as he handed Joseph to her and put his phone in his pocket. Kay handed Joseph to the assistant nurse so she could get Joseph cleaned up while she cleaned Beautiee up, the assistant nurse wrapped him up, and handed him to Beautiee...

"Hi Joseph..." Beautiee sighed...

"Okay – let's get you back to your room..." Kay said as she went to push the bed and Bazil tried to stop her... "I got it – but you can help steer from the head..."

"Got it..." Bazil said as they both steered the bed out of the delivery room and down the hall...

"Mommy!" Jay squealed when he saw Beautiee...

"Did you behave for Uncle Troy?" Bazil asked...

"Uh huh..."

"Good – you wanna meet your brother?"

"Yaaa!"

"Oh shit – Troy – get the doctor – Uggghh!" Keisha grunted as she grabbed Troy's hand and squeezed it...

"Keisha... I can't..."

"I'm standing right here!" Kay laughed...

"C'mon Jay – come meet your brother..." Bazil said as he took Jay and put Jay in the bed with Beautiee and Joseph... and Jay kissed him...

"Kay – these pains are getting... bad... Uggghh!"

"Let me take a look..." Kay said as she looked under the sheet...

"Hmmm – I still don't see the head – let me check to see if you've dilated..." she said as she examined Keisha... "Okay – you're fully dilated – time to push – let's go!"

"Oh thank God – I'ma kick your ass after I push this baby out Troy – Uggghh!"

"Why you wanna kick my ass Keisha?" Troy asked as he held her hand while Kay pushed the bed down the corridor to the delivery room...

"This baby's kickin' my ass – so I'm kickin' yours! Uggghh!"

"Hang on Keisha – we're just about there..." Kay said as she pushed the bed through the doors...

"Le'me get my phone..." Troy said...

"Troy – the baby..." Keisha panted...

"I got the phone – you get over there..." the nurse's assistant said as she took Troy's phone and started recording...

"Okay Keisha – push!" Kay yelled...

"Uuuuuggghhhh! Is he out yet?"

"Not yet..." Troy answered...

"Already getting' on my damn nerves – I ain't tryin'a lay up here pushing all night – you betta get your ass down there – Uuggghhh!"

"I see it! I see it!" Troy exclaimed...

"Okay Keisha – one more push should do it..."

"Uuugggghhhh!"

"You did it!" Kay exclaimed...

"Keisha..." Troy said as he picked up his child and then started crying...

"We have a girl?" Keisha asked excitedly...

"We have a baby girl..." Troy cried...

"Here Daddy – cut the cord..."Kay said as she handed Troy the scissors...

"I won't hurt her?"

"No Troy – go ahead..."

"Okay..." Troy said as he cut the cord... "Hi Amina..." he cried...

"Le'me hold her..." Keisha said. Troy went over to Keisha and gave Amina to her...

"Troy... she's so beautiful..."

"You're beautiful..." Troy said as he kissed her...

"I love you..."

"I love you too..."

"Here – take your phone – let me clean Amina up so you can go back to the room..." the nurse's assistant said as she put Troy's phone in his pocket and took Amina...

"We did it!" Keisha exclaimed...

"I told you!" Troy said...

"I know, I know – I owe you..."

"You ready to have another one?"

"Hell no!" Keisha laughed...

"Okay – we have a room for you and Beautiee so I'm gonna take you to your room – then we'll go get Beautiee..." Kay said...

"Okay..." Keisha said. Kay wheeled Keisha out the delivery room and down the corridor to their room and was surprised to see Beautiee...

"How'd you get in here?" she asked...

"Another nurse came by and told us our room was ready so here we are..." Bazil answered...

"Keisha – le'me see!" Beautiee said...

"Le'me see yours..." Keisha said...

"I'll take yours – Troy – you take ours..." Bazil said...

"Okay – hey little man..." Troy said as he went to pick up Joseph...

"No! My brother!" Jay said...

"I'm sorry Jay – can I see your brother? Please?"

"Okay..."

"Thank you Jay..." Troy said as he picked him up...

"Hey little man – what's your name?" Troy asked...

"Joseph..." Bazil answered...

"My brother Joseph..." Jay repeated...

"And who is this beautiful little girl?" Bazil asked...

"Amina..." Troy answered...

"Hi Amina..." Bazil said...

"Hello – can I see the baby?" Keisha laughed...

"Here..." Troy said as he gave Joseph to Keisha...

"Here..." Bazil said as he gave Amina to Beautiee...

"Bazil – I want another baby – I want a little girl – she's beautiful!" Beautiee exclaimed...

"I'on want another baby – but Joseph is cute – he looks just like his father..." Keisha said...

"My brother?" Jay asked...

"No Jay — that's my baby girl..." Troy said...

"Uncle Troy – baby girl!" Jay squealed...

"Troy — why you tell him that — now he thinks her name is Baby Girl!" Keisha laughed...

"Hi Starr — how are you feeling?" LuAnn asked as they got off the elevator....

"I'm... Uggghh!"

"Having a contraction — okay — let's get you to a bed — follow the nurse..." she said as Chandler pushed her... "How are you Theresa — are you okay?"

"I'm... Charles... Uggghh!"

"Also having contractions — okay — follow them — I'll be there in a few minutes..." LuAnn said as they all went down the hall to their room...

"Ladies — we need you to get undressed and put these gowns on — Mr. Corbett — pull the curtain there so you'll have privacy — hurry up if you can — the doctor will be here in a few minutes..." the nurse said as she left...

"You okay Theresa?" Charles asked...

"I'm okay... I'm just ready to... have... our... baby..." she grunted...

"Le'me help you outta these clothes and into your gown..." he said...

"Chandler... it hurts... Uggghh!" "Squeeze my hand... and breathe..." Chandler said as they started breathing together... "I'ma help you get into this gown – you keep breathing until the contraction passes..."

"Okay..." she panted..."

"Theresa – I'm going to check to see if you've dilated..." LuAnn said as she came into the room...

"Okay... Charles..."

"I'm here – take my hand..." he said as LuAnn looked under the sheet... "I don't see the head – I need to do an exam..."

"Okay..." Theresa panted...

"Okay – you've started dilating – but you're not ready to push yet – Starr – let's see how you're doing..." she said as she went over to Starr and looked under the sheet...

"I don't see the head – le'me do an exam and see what's going on..." she said as she started to do a pelvic exam...

"Is it going to hurt?" Starr asked...

"Starr – if you can handle labor – you can handle a pelvic exam – it won't hurt – I just need to see if you're dilating..." she said as she proceeded... "Hmmm... Mmmhmm... Chandler – I need to speak with you..."

"Is something wrong with my babies?" Starr asked with tears in her eyes...

"Starr – listen to me..." LuAnn said as she wiped Starr's tears... "Your babies are fine – okay?"

"Okay..."

"I just need to talk to Chandler – we'll be right outside – holler if you need me – or if another contraction hits..." she said as Chandler followed her out into the hallway... "Chandler – I'm a little concerned about Starr..."

"What's wrong?" Chandler asked as he started tearing up...

"Chandler..." she said as she took his hand... "Nothing's wrong – but I do have a concern..."

"Okay – what is it?"

"This is Starr's first pregnancy..."

"Okay..."

"She hasn't fully dilated..."

"Okay – but that's normal – right?"

"Yes – but what concerns me is that she could be in labor for hours – and the longer she's in labor, the harder the contractions hit..."

"Oh – okay – I'll help her through the contractions..."

"That's not all..."

"Okay – what else?"

"Earlier in her pregnancy, she fainted – right?"

"Yea..."

"She fainted because her blood pressure dropped..."

"Okay..."

"There's a chance that could happen while she's in labor – and that could put the babies in distress..."

"It could?"

"I need to let you know it's a possibility..."

"Okay..."

"It's also possible – based on the size of the babies – they may not fit in the birth canal..."

"I don't understand..."

"You're a big man – your babies are big – I would guess they'll be about 7 pounds..."

"Okay – so she can't push them out?"

"Honestly – I'm not sure – there's a chance she could have a normal delivery with no complications – but there's also a chance she could try to push – and then we'd need to do an emergency C-Section..."

"What should I do?"

"I recommend going for a C-Section rather than going through labor, contractions, and we end up having to do one anyway..."

"I'll do whatever my wife wants to do..."

"Okay – let me check on Theresa while you talk to Starr..." she said and then they both went back in the room... "How's it going?" LuAnn asked...

"We've been having contractions – but we're helping each other..." Starr answered...

"Yea – we take turns squeezing each other's hand..." Theresa laughed...

"Okay – I'm going to check you both again – Starr – let me start with you..." she said as she looked under the sheet and did a pelvic exam... "Hmmm – okay – Theresa – let's see how you're doing..." she said as she proceeded to do a pelvic exam... "Oh my goodness – you're ready – let's get you to delivery!" she exclaimed...

"I am? Oh my God! Charles..."

"I know baby – I know..." he said as he kissed her and LuAnn proceeded to push the bed down to the delivery room...

"Chandler..." Starr whispered as she started to cry...

"Uh uh! Stop that..." he said as he kissed her...

"What's wrong?"

"Nothing is wrong – the babies are fine..."

"You promise?"

"I promise..."

"So why did LuAnn want to talk to you?"

"LuAnn said she doesn't want your blood pressure to drop while you're in labor – she says it will put the babies in distress..."

"I thought you said the babies are fine?"

"They are – LuAnn just wants them to stay that way..."

"Okay – what else?"

"LuAnn said the babies will be about 7 pounds each..."

"Oh my God!"

"She said you might not be able to push them out..."

"What are we supposed to do?"

"LuAnn wants to do a C-Section..."

"Why?"

"LuAnn doesn't want you to go through labor and then you wind up needing an emergency C-Section..."

"I don't want that either..."

"So you'll do the C-Section?"

"Yea..."

"Good – I was hoping you'd say that..."

"I'll take your phone – you get down there and watch your child come into the world..." the nurse's assistant said as she took Charles' phone and started recording...

"Uggghh! Can I push now?" Theresa grunted...

"Yes! Push!" LuAnn said...

"Uggghh!"

"Baby – I see him! I see him!" Charles said as he started jumping up and down...

"One more push should do it – are you ready Theresa?"

"Hell yea I'm ready – Uuuggghhh!"

"Baby – he's almost out!"

"Charles – see if you can help him out..." LuAnn said...

"C'mon son – Daddy's here..." Charles said as he helped his son slide into the world...

"Congratulations..." LuAnn said...

"We have a son..." Charles said as he started crying...

"Okay Charles – I need you to steady your hand so you can cut the cord..." LuAnn said as she handed Charles the scissors and his son started to cry...

"Am I hurting him?"

"No Charles – go on – cut the cord..."

"Okay..." Charles cried as he cut the cord... "You're so beautiful..." Charles cried as he kissed his bloody forehead...

"Charles – give him to me..." Theresa said...

"Here's Mommy..." Charles said as he handed their son to her...

"Oh Charles... we have a son..."

"We have a son..." Charles cried as he kissed her...

"I love you so much..."

"I love you too..." he breathed as he kissed her again...

"Okay – I need you to take this..." the nurse's assistant said as she put Charles' phone in his pocket... "and I'll take him..." she said as she reached out to take the baby...

"Okay – here he is..." Charles said as he gave his son to her. They watched as the nurse's assistant cleaned him up and wrapped him in a blanket... "There – all better – you can go with your parents now..." she said as she handed the baby to Charles...

"Hey son…" Charles said as he took him and kissed his forehead… "Here's your mother…" he said as he gave him to Theresa…

"Okay – let's get you into your room – then I'll go get Starr…" LuAnn said as she wheeled the bed out of the delivery room, down the hall, and into their room…

"Where's Starr?" Theresa asked…

"She's still in the other room – you'll see her in a while…" LuAnn said as she went to go get Starr…

"Hello Starr – are you still having contractions?"

"Yes she is…" Chandler answered…

"Okay – did Chandler tell you what we spoke about?"

"Yes I did…" Chandler answered…

"Chandler – I need to hear it from her…"

"Yes – he told me – I'll do it…"

"Okay – I need to let you know there are risks…"

"Okay – what are they?"

"They'll be a lot of bleeding – you could develop blood clots – your babies may have trouble breathing – there's an increased risk for future pregnancies – you could get an infection – your babies could get injured – other organs could get inured – you have a longer recovery time – you could have adhesions – and you could have hernias…"

"Chandler... I'm scared..." Starr said as she started to cry...

"LuAnn – all of that can happen?" Chandler asked as he took Starr's hand...

"I don't mean all of it – I have to tell you everything that could happen..."

"Okay..."

"I'll do it..."

"You sure?" Chandler asked...

"Yea – if I can't push them out I'll have to have a C-Section anyway... oh boy... here comes another one... Uggghh!" she grunted as she squeezed Chandler's hand...

"Okay – now I need to explain the procedure..." LuAnn said...

"Okay..." They both said in unison...

"I'll clean your abdomen, you'll get an IV, and a catheter..."

"A catheter?" Starr asked...

"Yes – we need to make sure your bladder stays empty during the surgery..."

"How long do I have to keep it in?"

"At least 24 hours..."

"Okay..." she sighed...

"Now we need to talk about the anesthesia..."

"Okay..." they both said in unison...

"The spinal block is injected into the sack that surrounds your spinal cord – it numbs your lower body..."

"So I can't move at all?" Starr asked...

"Right..."

"I don't think I want that one – what else?"

"The epidural is the most common for vaginal and cesarean deliveries – it's injected into your lower back outside the sac of your spinal cord..."

"Okay..." they both said in unison...

"General anesthesia puts you to sleep – we only use that for emergencies..."

"I don't want to be asleep – I wanna stay awake!" Starr exclaimed...

"So you want the epidural?"

"Yes..."

"Okay – now I need to explain the surgery..."

"Chandler... oh God... it hurts... Uggghh!"

"Breathe Starr..." Chandler said as he breathed along with Starr...

"Okay – I'm going to cut your abdomen – then I'll cut your uterus – then I'll take your babies out – the staff will make sure your babies are breathing properly - they'll clamp and cut the umbilical cords - they'll clear their noses and mouths of fluids – they'll clean 'em up – and they'll give them to you..."

"How long do I have to stay in the hospital?"

"Three to four days..."

"Can I breast-feed?"

"Yes – you can breast feed – but I need to discuss something else with you..."

"Okay..."

"Do you want more children?"

"Yes – I want more children..." Starr sighed. Chandler took Starr's hand and kissed it...

"If you decide you want more children – you'll have to have a C-Section every time you get pregnant..."

"I will?"

"Yes – and each pregnancy will have the same risks..."

"What do you think I should do?"

"Oh Starr – I can't answer that for you – what I can tell you is that you're young – you're healthy – but you need to heal from this surgery before you even think about getting pregnant again..."

"Oh boy – I don't know what to do Chandler..."

"What if we don't have any more children?" Chandler asked...

"If you're sure you don't want any more children – I can tie her tubes while I have her open..."

"I don't wanna tie my tubes yet – I wanna have another baby!"

"Starr..." Chandler said as he started to cry... "You don't have to do this for me – I have my girls – I have you – that's enough..."

"No it isn't – I want to... oh God... Uggghh!"

"Okay – I get it – you want more children – I won't tie your tubes – let's go!" LuAnn ordered as she wheeled the bed down to the delivery room... "Okay – before I do anything – I need all of these forms signed..." she said as she handed Starr about 12 pages attached to a clip board. Luann waited for Starr to sign all the forms and then she proceeded... "Okay Starr – we're going to put in the IV..."

"Chandler..."

"I'm right here..." Chandler said as he took her hand and the nurse put the IV in Starr's arm...

"Okay Starr – turn on your side – and be perfectly still – you're going to feel a pinch..."

"Owww!"

"You're doing great Starr – don't move – almost done – okay – now let's bring your babies into the world..." LuAnn said as she cleaned Starr's abdomen and Chandler began recording...

"Let me get that..." the nurse's assistant said – put this gown and gloves on so you can hold your babies..."

"Okay..." Chandler said as he gave her the phone, took the gown and gloves, and put them on...

"I'm going to cut you now..." LuAnn said as she began cutting Starr's abdomen...

"You okay Starr?" she asked as Chandler took Starr's hand...

"I'm okay..."

"Good – I'm going to cut your uterus now… oh my goodness – here's your first child…" she said as she took out their first baby…"

"Kalliyah…" Chandler said as he started to cry…

"Kalliyah… I like that – who does she look like Chandler?"

"She looks like you…" Chandler answered…

"Here's your second child…" LuAnn said as she took out their second baby…

"Chelsea…" Starr said…

"Chelsea… I like that…"

"Chandler…"

"Yes Starr…"

"I love you…"

"I love you too…" he said as he bent down to kiss her…

"Okay – it'll be a few more minutes – I need to close you up…" LuAnn said as she proceeded… "Okay ‐ you're all done – the catheter will stay in you for tonight – I'm going to sit you up now so you can see your girls…" she said as she sat the bed up…

"Hey Kalliyah, hey Chelsea…" Chandler said as he held his daughters…

"Chandler – how can you tell them apart?"

"This is Kalliyah… and this is Chelsea…" he said as he gave them to her to hold…

"Oh my God – Chelsea – you have my eyes!" Starr whispered…

"Okay – I need to give you your phone now..." the nurse's assistant laughed as she stopped recording and put Chandler's phone in his pocket... "Otherwise we'll be here all night..."

"Okay – let's get you in your room so you and your babies can get some rest..." LuAnn said as she wheeled the bed out the delivery room and down the hallway to their room...

"Starr! Chandler! Congratulations!" Charles exclaimed...

"Congratulations to you too!" Chandler exclaimed... "What'd you have?"

"We have a son..." Theresa beamed...

"Le'me see..." Chandler said as he went over to take a look... "Hey Charles – I'm Uncle Chandler..." he said as he picked up their son... "Come meet your Aunt Starr – and your cousin's Kalliyah and Chelsea..." he said as he placed the baby with Starr...

"Aww... this is how it'll be when I give you a son..." she said...

"Starr? Are you kidding me? You want another baby?" Theresa asked...

"Chandler and I both want another baby – right?" she asked, looking at Chandler...

"Yea..." Chandler sighed...

"God bless y'all – maybe we can try again too..." Charles said...

"Charles – unless you plan on carrying the next one – I'ma need you to pump the breaks..." Theresa laughed...

"Le'me see my Kalliyah and my Chelsea..." Charles said as he went over to Starr... "Oh my God – Chandler – Starr – your daughters are beautiful! Can I pick them up?"

"Go 'head Uncle Charles..." Chandler laughed...

"Which one is Kalliyah?"

"This one..." Chandler said as he picked her up and handed her to Charles...

"Theresa – look at her!" Charles exclaimed as he gave Kalliyah to her...

"She looks just like you Chandler!" Theresa exclaimed...

"And this is Chelsea..." Chandler said as he picked Chelsea up and handed her to Charles...

"No! Theresa – look!" he exclaimed as he handed Chelsea to her...

"Oh my God! She has blue eyes like Starr! Oh wow!" Theresa exclaimed...

"Okay – let's give them back to their mother's... Chandler said as he gave Theresa back her son and then gave Starr Kalliyah and Chelsea...

"Starr?" Theresa asked... "You okay?"

"Yea..."

"You sure?"

"Yea..."

"Why do you have an IV?"

"I had a C-Section..."

"Oh my God! Are you in any pain?"

"A little..."

"You're in pain and you still want another baby – you must really love Chandler..."

"I do..."

"I love you too..." Chandler said as he kissed her...

"Okay Mary – let's get you into the room so you can change into a gown and we'll see how you're doing..." Dr. Melanie Ornstein said as they went into the room...

"You okay Mary?" Wayne asked...

"I'm fine..." Mary sighed...

"Let me help you..." Wayne said as he helped Mary up onto the bed and then began undressing her...

"Wayne... stop..." she laughed...

"No..." he said as he lifted her top over her head and proceeded to unhook her bra... "You look so beautiful..." he sighed as he stood back and admired her...

"Thank you..."

"Here – let me help you put this on..." he said as he helped her put the gown on. Once she had the gown on, he lifted her legs up into the bed, laid her on her back, lifted her gown, and proceeded to remove her panties...

"Wayne.... Stop it!" Mary laughed...

"Hello baby..." he said as he kissed Mary's stomach... "I can't wait to meet you..." he said as he slid Mary's panties off and then spread her legs...

"Wayne!"

"Relax... I'm just looking..."

"I remember you did the same thing when I was pregnant with Starr..." Mary laughed...

"Me too..." Wayne laughed...

"And we almost got caught..." he laughed...

"Exactly – that's why you need to stop..." she laughed...

"How are we doing in here?" Melanie asked...

"I'm okay so far – I'm just ready to have our baby..." Mary answered...

"Are you having contractions?"

"I was – but I haven't had one in a while – ooops – I spoke too soon..." Mary grunted as Wayne took her hand and she squeezed it...

"Let me see what's happening..." Melanie said as she looked under Mary's gown... "I don't see the head – let's see if you've dilated any..." she said as she examined Mary... "Oh wow – you'll be ready to push soon..."

"Really? Oh wow – Wayne!"

"I know Mommy..." he said as he kissed her...

"I'll be back in a bit..." Melanie said as she left the room...

"I wonder how Starr's doing?" Mary asked...

"Let's call them..." Wayne said as he called Chandler...

"Hey Wayne — I've been trying to call you..."

"Is everything okay?"

"Starr had the babies!"

"Hold on..." Wayne said as he put the phone on speaker... "Chandler says Starr had the babies..."

"What? Oh my God — why didn't you call us? How is she?" Mary exclaimed...

"Starr..."

"Huh?"

"Your mother's on the phone..."

"Hi Mommy..."

"Starr! Are you okay?"

"I had a C-Section..."

"Oh my God! Is everything alright?"

"You wanna see?"

"Yea — le'me see..."

"Chandler — put this on face-time so Mommy can see..."

"Hey y'all..." Chandler said after putting the phone on face-time...

"Oh Wayne — look at our beautiful grandbabies..." Mary whispered as she started crying...

"Congratulations Chandler..." Wayne said...

"Mommy – are you in the hospital?" Starr asked...

"Yea..."

"Oh my God – Mommy – you're in labor too?" Starr squealed...

"Yes baby..."

"Hi Wayne – Hi Mary..." Theresa said...

"Who's that?" Wayne asked...

"That's Theresa Mommy!" Starr squealed...

"Oh my God – all our babies will have the same birthday!" Mary laughed...

"Congratulations Charles..." Wayne said...

"Congratulations to you too – well – not yet..." Charles laughed...

"Oh God – Wayne – here comes another one – I think it's time – Starr – call your father – Uggghh!"

"Okay Mommy – I love you..."

"I... love... you... too... Uggghh!"

"I'll get the doctor now..." Wayne said as Melanie came in...

"Is she having contractions?"

"Yea..."

"Le'me take a look..." she said as she looked under Mary's gown...

"Oh boy – she's ready – let's have a baby!" Melanie said as she wheeled Mary out the room and down the hall to the delivery room...

"Starr – Beautiee had the baby..." Bazil said as he answered the phone...

"Oh my God – when?"

"A few hours ago…"

"Daddy…"

"What's wrong Starr?"

"Hey Daddy…" Chandler said as he took the phone…

"Hey Chandler – everything okay?"

"Hold on – le'me face-time y'all" Chandler said… "Say high to Grandpa and Grandma…" Chandler said as he put the camera on his daughters…

"Oh my God – they're beautiful…" Bazil whispered as he cried…

"Look at our beautiful grandbabies…" Beautiee said…

"Beautiee – is that Jay? And my new baby brother?" Starr asked…

"Starr – my brother – Joseph!" Jay squealed…

"Hi Jay! Hi Joseph! This is your Aunt Kalliyah and this is your Aunt Chelsea…"

"Aunty Kay Kay – Chelsea!" Jay squealed…

"Hey y'all!" Charles said…

"Who's that?" Bazil asked…

"It's Charles!" "And Theresa!"

"Congratulations!" Beautiee said… "What'd you have?"

"We have a son!" Charles beamed…

"So – who's the oldest?" Chandler asked…

"We had Joseph a few hours ago..." Beautiee answered...

"We had Charles right before Starr had Kalliyah and Chelsea..." Theresa answered...

"So our baby is the oldest – then Theresa – then Starr – Starr?"

"Yes Beautiee?"

"Where's your mother?"

"She's in the hospital – she's in labor too!" Starr laughed...

"Okay Mary – push!" Melanie said...

"Wait a minute..." Mary panted...

"I'm recording – go ahead and push!" the nurse's assistant laughed...

"Uggghh!"

"Mary – I see hair!" Wayne said excitedly...

"Okay Daddy – go help your baby into the world..." Melanie said...

"Mary – help Wayne help your baby – push!"

"Uuuugggghhhh!"

"Oh my God – my Sky!" Wayne whispered as he cried...

"We have a girl?"

"We have another girl..." Wayne said as he brought Sky over to Mary and laid her on Mary's chest...

"Sky..." Mary cried...

"Daddy – we need to cut the cord – and we need to clean her up..." Melanie said as she handed Wayne the scissors... "Okay – good job Daddy – now they can get her cleaned up..." Melanie said as she cleaned Mary up...

"Wayne..." Mary whispered...

"Yes Mommy?" Wayne answered with a smile...

"Come closer..." she whispered...

"Okay..." he whispered as he bent over her...

"Sky is so white..." she laughed...

"She is a little pale..." Wayne laughed...

"Wayne – I don't think she's Jermoll's baby..."

"Mary – it doesn't matter – I love you – I love her..."

"I want a paternity test..."

"Are you sure that's what you want?"

"Yes..."

"Mary – let's just be happy – it doesn't matter – I swear..."

"Wayne – I have a feeling..."

"Are you sure?"

"Yes – I'm sure..."

"Okay..." Wayne sighed... "If that's what you want..." he said as he kissed her...

"Here's your baby girl..." the nurse's assistant said as she handed Sky to Wayne... "And here's your phone..." she said as she put the phone back in his pocket...

"Are you ready to go back to your room?" Melanie asked...

"Yes – I'm ready..." Mary answered...

"Okay!" Melanie said as she went to wheel the bed out of the delivery room and Wayne stopped her...

"I'll get it..."

"Thank you Wayne – I'll show you where your room is..." she said as she led the way. When they got to their room Melanie made sure they were settled before she started to leave...

"Melanie?" Mary asked...

"Yes?"

"We need a paternity test..."

"Umm... I see... ummm... well..."

"It's okay Melanie..." Wayne said... "My wife was in a relationship before we got back together and she got pregnant around the time we got back together..."

"Oh thank God – I've had this situation once before with another patient – and it wasn't pretty..."

"What happened?" Mary asked...

"Her husband left her here in the hospital..." Melanie sighed...

"Oh my God..."

"I'll never leave you – no matter what..." Wayne said as he kissed Mary...

"Aww... how sweet – is Sky sleeping?"

"Yea – she's sleeping..." Mary answered...

"Okay – I'll be right back..." Melanie said as she left the room...

"Mary – you don't have to do this... I promise..."

"I love you so much – if there's a possibility... I wanna know..."

"I love you too – and it doesn't matter..."

"Okay Wayne – open your mouth..." Melanie said. Wayne opened his mouth and Melanie swabbed the inside of his cheek and put the swab in a bag... "Now for Sky..." she said as she gently opened Sky's mouth, swabbed her cheek, and put the swab in a separate bag... "I'll get this to the lab – if it's not busy - you'll know in 24 hours..."

"Thank you Melanie..." Mary sighed...

"You're welcome – and congratulations..." she said as she left...

"Good evening..." the security guard said as he came into Beautiee and Keisha's room...

"Hello..." they all said in unison...

"Visiting hours are over..." he said...

"We're the parents..." Troy said...

"Congratulations – but – as I said – visiting hours are over..."

"I'm spending the night..." Troy said as he climbed in bed beside Keisha...

"Sir... please..." the security guard sighed...

"I'm aaight Troy – I'll see you tomorrow..." Keisha said...

"Beautiee? You okay?" Bazil asked...

"I'm okay – it's not like you can stay anyway..." Beautiee laughed...

"Mr. Osgood? Is that you?" the security guard asked as Bazil turned around...

"I'm Mr. Osgood..." Bazil answered...

"Oh my God – it's a pleasure to meet you!" he exclaimed as he grabbed Bazil's hand and shook it vigorously before Bazil could offer it...

"Thank you..." Bazil laughed...

"Congratulations – is this your wife?" he asked...

"Yes – and these are my friends – but – as you said – we need to get going... so we'll see you another time..." Bazil answered, hinting for him to leave...

"Oh – sorry – my bad – I didn't mean to disturb y'all..." he said as he left...

"No! I want Mommy!" Jay said...

"Jay – Mommy's tired – go home with Daddy – I'll see you when you wake up..." I yawned...

"My brother come with Daddy?"

"No Jay – Joseph will see you tomorrow too..."

"Good night Keisha, good night Amina..." Troy said as he kissed them both...

"Baby girl – Amina..." Jay said...

"That's right Jay..." Keisha said...

"I love you..." Bazil said as he kissed Beautiee...

"I love you more..." Beautiee said as she kissed him back...

"I love you Joseph..." Bazil said as he kissed him...

"Daddy love Jay?" Jay asked...

"I love you Jay..." Bazil said as he picked Jay up and kissed him...

"Come give Mommy a kiss Jay..." Beautiee said...

"I love you Mommy..." Jay said as he kissed Beautiee...

"I love you more..." Beautiee said as she kissed him back...

"I love you Joseph..." Jay said as he kissed him...

"C'mon Troy – let's go home and get a nap in – tomorrow comes quick..." Bazil said...

"You ain't neva lie!" Troy laughed...

"Good evening – visiting hours are over..." the security guard said as he walked into Starr and Theresa's room...

"I didn't know they had visiting hours at 2 a.m....." Charles laughed...

"Hello Sergeant..." the security guard said to Chandler...

"Hello... do I know you?"

"I've seen you in here before..."

"Oh... okay..."

"Congratulations – what'd you have?"

"We have twin girls – and my best friend has a son..."

"Oh wow – that's nice – I guess y'all get along really well..."

"We do..." Starr said...

"Can I see the babies?"

"You can look..." Chandler said...

"I understand – especially 'cause I haven't washed my hands..." he said as he looked at the twins... "Oh my goodness – they look just like you..."

"Thank you..." Chandler said...

"And this must be your son – you sure can't deny him..." he said to Charles...

"Thank you..." Charles said...

"You staying Sergeant?" he asked Chandler...

"I might..." Chandler answered...

"Alright then – congratulations Moms and Dads..." he said as he left the room...

"It's okay Charles – you can go get some sleep..." Theresa said...

"You sure?"

"Yea – might as well get some now – 'cause I'm not letting you get any sleep once we get home..." she laughed...

"That's fine with me..." Charles said as he kissed her...

"I love you..."

"I love you too..."

"I love you son..." Charles said as he kissed his son...

"Starr – you okay?"

"I'm sleepy..." she slurred...

"Oh she got that good shit goin' in that IV..." Theresa laughed...

"I'ma go with Charles and get some sleep – I'll see you in the morning..." Chandler said as he kissed her...

"I love you..."

"I love you too..."

"I love y'all..." he said as he kissed the twins...

"Look y'all – she sleep..." Theresa said as she pointed at Starr...

"Excuse me sir – visiting hours are over..." the security guard said as he came into Mary's room...

"I'm staying..." Wayne said...

"I hear ya..."

"That was easy..." Wayne laughed...

"I stayed with mine too..."

"How many do you have?"

"I have one – a son..."

"Aww... that's nice..."

"How many do you have?"

"Two – both girls – this is our second..." Wayne said as he looked over at Mary...

"Congratulations – she's cute..."

"Thank you..." Mary said...

"I gotta make rounds – congratulations again..." he said as he left the room...

"You okay Mary?"

"I'm fine..." Mary yawned... "Are you really staying? You can go if you want..."

"I can't – it won't feel right without you and Sky..."

"Aww... I love you so much..."

"I love you too... both of you..." he said as he kissed them both...

"C'mon Jay – let's go night night..." Bazil said as he put Jay in his crib... and Jay started to cry... "What's wrong Jay?"

"I want Mommy..."

"You wanna come sleep with Daddy?"

"Uh huh..."

"C'mon..." Bazil said as he took him into their bedroom and as soon as Bazil laid him down, he was fast asleep...

"I heard Jay – he aiight?" Troy asked...

"He's fine – he just wants his mother – I put him in our bed – he's already asleep..."

"Aiight – I'ma get a nap in while I can – good night..." he said as he gave Bazil a hug...

"Good night – I love you man..."

"I love you too..."

"We're here…" Charles said as they got off the elevator…

"Yes we are…" Chandler agreed…

"Thank you Chandler…"

"For what?"

"A year ago my wife wanted a divorce – now look at us…"

"I'm happy for y'all…"

"Thank God you and Starr came along when you did – who knows what would've happened…"

"I feel the same way about Starr – the crazy thing is – I almost broke up with her…" Chandler laughed…

"You lyin'! What happened?"

"Another story for another time – I need some sleep… good night…" Chandler yawned…

"Good night – I'll knock later on…" Charles said.

Chapter FOUR

"Good morning Beautiee – good morning Keisha – how are you feeling?" Kay asked as she came in the room…

"I'm ready to go home!" Keisha laughed…

"I guess you're ready to go too Beautiee?"

"Yes I am!"

"I looked over your charts – you're both good – the babies are fine – I'll get you both discharged – but you can't leave until your husband's get here – and you must be in a wheelchair!"

"Aiight – damn!" Keisha laughed…

"Keisha – Beautiee – as long as you're in the hospital – we're responsible for you – that means if you stub your toe on the way out – we're responsible – what if you tripped and dropped your baby..."

"Kay! Calm down!" Beautiee said...

"I'm sorry - I didn't mean to take it out on you – sometimes – I swear – it's like talkin' to fuckin' kids – never mind..."

"Kay – come – sit..." Keisha said as she patted her bed and Kay sat down, and sighed...

"You ladies are blessed – you have husbands – but some of these young girls – you try to talk to them and they're so quick to get an attitude..."

"I know what you mean – I've had a few of those..." Beautiee laughed...

"I'm their doctor – I'm only telling them for their own good – but noooo – they're so fuckin' smart – like that lil' bitch down there hollerin'..."

"Oh shit!" Keisha exclaimed...

"I should let her go through that shit – but I'ma give her an epidural to make it easier for her..."

"You nice – most doctors won't give a shit unless it's a matter of life-or-death..." Beautiee said...

"I'll let you in on a secret..." Kay whispered...

"Okay – what?" Keisha whispered...

"It depends on your insurance – that lil' bitch down there only has Medicaid – Medicaid doesn't even cover it – but I'ma give it to her and code it so Medicaid will pay for it..."

"Aww – see – that's what I'm talkin' about!" Keisha said...

"Okay ladies – I got babies to deliver – get dressed – get those babies dressed – I'll see you both in six weeks – and Beautiee?"

"I know, I know!" Beautiee laughed...

"She ain't gonna listen Kay – hell – I might not either!" Keisha laughed...

"I can't – I gotta go!" Kay said as she turned to leave and ran right into Bazil, Jay, and Troy...

"Hi guys – bye guys – I got babies to deliver..." she said as she left...

"Everything alright?" Troy asked...

"We ready!" Keisha said as she jumped down off the bed and pulled him into a kiss...

"Mmm... okay..." Troy said as he pulled the curtain to give them some privacy...

"Mommy!" Jay squealed... "Mommy – up-up..."

"Mommy can't pick you up Jay – she just had a baby..."

"Bazil – you pick him up and I can hug him on the bed..." Beautiee said...

"C'mon Jay..." Bazil said as he picked Jay up and put him on the bed beside Beautiee...

"How's my big boy?" Beautiee asked as she hugged Jay and held him...

"I'm fine..."

"You wanna hold your brother?"

"Okay!" Jay beamed...

"Here..." Beautiee said as she picked up Joseph out of the basinet and placed him on Jay's lap...

"Put this arm here... and this arm here..." she said as she helped Jay hold his brother...

"Aww – that's a beautiful picture..." Bazil said as he took out his phone and took the picture...

"Okay Jay – Mommy's gonna put your brother in the basinet – you sit in the chair – we're gonna get dressed and then we can go home – okay?"

"Okay Mommy..." Jay said as Beautiee took the baby and Jay waited for Bazil to put him in the chair...

"I'm gonna help your mother get dressed..." Bazil said as he pulled the curtain and then pulled her into a kiss...

"I can't wait to get home..."

"I can't wait to get you home..."

"Le'me hurry up..." Beautiee sighed as she started getting dressed. When she was done Bazil pulled back the curtain... "Why you smiling at me like that?" Beautiee asked...

"Nothing..." Keisha smiled back mischievously...

"Let go home..." Bazil said as he picked up Joseph...

"Uh uh – Kay said wheelchairs – she was already yellin' at us!" Beautiee laughed...

"C'mon Troy – let's go get them wheelchairs..." Bazil laughed as they both left the room...

"Good morning!" LuAnn said as she walked into Starr and Theresa's room...

"Good morning!" Theresa beamed...

"Morning..." Starr mumbled...

"What's wrong?" LuAnn asked...

"I wanna go home..." she sighed...

"Aww – I'll come visit you Starr..." Theresa said...

"Thanks – but I won't be here that long – besides – you should be with your baby..." she sighed...

"I know you're going to miss your friend – but you'll have your babies with you..." LuAnn said...

"That's true..." Starr agreed as she perked up a bit...

"Okay then – Theresa – I'm going to get your discharge papers ready – you can leave when your husband gets here – and you must be in a wheelchair – okay?"

"Okay LuAnn..." Theresa agreed...

"Okay Starr - I'm going to take a look at your staples..."

"Staples? Oh my God! I was stapled?"

"Yes Starr – you were stapled – but the staples will be removed before you go home..."

"Will it hurt?"

"No..."

"You promise?"

"Starr..." LuAnn said as she took Starr's hand... "I'll always be up-front with you..."

"Okay — can I at least get this catheter out?"

"Yes..."

"Thank you Lord!

"Okay — let's take a look..." she said as she pulled the curtain and lifted Starr's gown... "Everything looks good..."

"So I can get them out?"

"Not yet — we can't risk your wound opening up and then we have to re-staple you again..."

"Good morning!" Chandler boomed as he walked in with Charles...

"Good morning beautiful..." Charles said as he walked over to Theresa and kissed her...

"Good morning..."

"Where's Charles?"

"He's over there in the basinet..."

"Good morning son..." Charles said as he picked his son up and kissed him...

"You can dress him while I get dressed..."

"You're going home?"

"Yes we are..." Theresa said as she pulled the curtain so she could get dressed...

"How's my wife?" Chandler asked LuAnn...

"I wanna go home... but I can't..." Starr sighed...

"I'll come be with you every day until you can come home..." Chandler said as he kissed her and rubbed his hand over her stomach...

"Chandler – I got stapled..."

"Really?"

"Let me show you..." LuAnn said as she lifted Starr's gown up..."

"Wow... do they hurt?"

"No..."

"We'll remove the staples before she leaves – but today – she can get that catheter out – then we're gonna get you up outta bed and have you walk around – it'll keep you from getting blood clots..." LuAnn said...

"I get to get outta bed? I get to walk around with no catheter? I get to pee on the toilet? Woo hoo! Ouch..."

"Easy Starr..." Chandler said...

"I'm ready – can I go now?" Theresa asked...

"I haven't had a chance to prepare your discharge papers – you can follow me down to the nurse's station and leave from there – Charles – your wife needs to be in a wheelchair – understand?"

"Yes Maam – bye y'all!" Charles said...

"Well damn – bye to you too!" Chandler snapped...

"I'm sorry – I just can't wait to get home with my wife and my son..."

"I'm just playin' – go 'head – I'll stop by later tonight..."

"Aiight – later..." Charles said as he left out the room...

"Bye Theresa – bye Charles..." Starr said...

"You okay Starr?" Theresa asked...

"I'll be fine – I thought I was gonna have to stay in bed – I can go get my babies – and I can eat..." Starr answered as she smiled...

"You're smiling – I can go now..." Theresa said...

"Oh so I don't have nothin' to do with you smiling – fine then – I'll leave with them..." Chandler said...

"Chandler!" Starr sighed...

"I'm just playing..." Chandler laughed...

"Bye y'all..." Theresa said as she left the room and the nurse came in...

"Good morning – I'm here to remove your catheter..."

"Go right ahead!" Starr beamed as she pulled up her gown and spread her legs open...

"Okay..." the nurse laughed... "I guess you're ready to get it out..." she laughed as she went between Starr's legs and took it out... "I'm done – you can close your legs now..." the nurse said as she gathered the catheter, the tubes, and left the room...

"How do I look Chandler?' Starr asked...

"Now see – you startin' trouble..." Chandler laughed as he looked between her legs...

"Six weeks is a long time..."

"We can come up with something..." he said as he rubbed her thigh...

"Help me up – I wanna go see my babies..."

"Your babies?"

"Our babies – they're probably hungry..."

"I'm sure they are – speaking of hungry – have you eaten yet?"

"Nope..."

"C'mon – let's go..." he said as he eased her up gently and she stood up...

"I love you Chandler..."

"I love you too..." he said as he pulled her into a hug and held her...

"You feel good..."

"See – you startin' trouble again..." Chandler laughed...

"Let's go..." Starr said as she took a couple of steps...

"You okay?"

"Yea – help me with the IV..."

"Okay – what side do you want it on?"

"Doesn't matter..."

"Okay – you walk – I'll roll it beside you..." he said as they went down the hall towards the maternity ward...

"Good morning..." Wayne yawned as he woke up to Mary breast-feeding Sky..."

"Good morning..." Mary said...

"You look so beautiful..." Wayne said...

"You hear that Sky? Daddy says we're beautiful..."

"You are..." Wayne said as he took out his phone and took a picture...

"I can't wait to go home..."

"Neither can I..."

"Good morning – how are you guys doing?" Melanie said as she walked in...

"We're fine..." Mary answered...

"Aww... your daughter has a healthy appetite I see..."

"Yes she does – just like her father..." Mary laughed...

'Speaking of that... I have the results of the paternity test..."

"Okay..." Wayne said...

"Here – read it and see for yourself..." she said as she handed the paper to Wayne. Wayne read the results as Mary waited anxiously. He didn't say anything – he just burst into tears...

"Wayne – I'm sorry..." Mary whispered as she started to cry...

"She's mine..." Wayne cried...

"Wait – what?"

"She's mine – Sky's my daughter..."

"Oh my God... we have a baby?"

"Yes Mary – we have a baby..." Wayne cried as he kissed her hard... "Thank you Lord... Thank you..." Wayne cried...

"You're welcome..." God said...

"I'm so happy for you both..." Melanie said...

"You don't understand..." Wayne cried...

"Miracles happen every day..." Melanie said...

"Yes they do..." Mary cried...

"I'm your Daddy Sky..." Wayne cried as he kissed her...

"I'll go get your discharge papers ready – get dressed – you can leave whenever you like – but you must be in a wheelchair – got it?"

"Got it..." they both said in unison...

"I love you..." Wayne said as he kissed Mary again...

"I love you too..." Mary said as she kissed him back.

FIVE

One Year Later...

"Mommy! She hit me!"

"You hit me first!

"I'ma 'bout to hit both'a y'all!" Chandler yelled...

"Might as well get up now..." Starr sighed as she tried to get up and fell back on the bed...

"I'll help you..." Chandler said as he got up out the bed, went over to Starr, puller her up off the bed into a hug, and kissed her...

"I feel like I'm having twins again..." Starr sighed...

"You look just as beautiful as you did when you were pregnant the first time..." Chandler said as he held her...

"I'm so tired... I wish I could go back to bed..."

"You can..."

"No I can't – we have too much to do..." she sighed...

"You can go back to bed – I'll make coffee – I'll feed the kids – you don't have to get up until everyone gets here..."

"You sure?"

"Starr – I got it..."

"Okay... I'm gonna lay back down..." she yawned...

"Kalliyah – Chelsea – c'mon in the kitchen so you can eat..."

"Okay Daddy..." they said as they followed him into the kitchen...

"No! I wanna sit there! Daddy – she pushed me!" Kalliyah whined..."

"Chelsea – you got one more time..."

"I didn't do anything!"

"Kalliyah – come sit here..."

"Thank you Daddy..."

"Chelsea – you sit over there..."

"Hmmph!" she said as she sat in the other seat...

"Whatchall want for breakfast?"

"I want French toast!" Kalliyah squealed...

"Me too!" Chelsea squealed...

"Okay – I'ma make your mother some coffee – and I'ma make you some French toast – but I need y'all to do something for me..."

"Yes Daddy?" they both said in unison...

"I need y'all to behave so you can get those presents under the tree..."

"I want presents!" Kalliyah squealed...

"Me too!" Chelsea squealed...

"You can have them later – but you need to behave...

"I'm bein' have Daddy..." Kalliyah said...

"I'm bein' have too..." Chelsea said...

"I'ma take this coffee in to your mother – I'll be right back..." Chandler said as he left them in the kitchen and went to bring Starr coffee... "Starr? Starr? You awake?"

"No..."

"I brought you some coffee..."

"Thank you..." Starr yawned. Chandler put the coffee down on the nightstand, went over to Starr, and helped her sit up...

"I'm sorry..." Starr sighed...

"What'd I tell you about apologizing?"

"I'm sorry Chandler..."

"Here – drink your coffee..."

"Okay..." she said as she started drinking the coffee...

"Daddy! We're hungry!" Chelsea yelled...

"I'm coming..." Chandler said as he hurried back into the kitchen. Starr finished her coffee, put the cup back on the nightstand, laid back down, and went back to sleep... "Aiight – y'all ready?" Chandler asked...

"Yaaaa!" they answered in unison...

"Who wants juice?"

"Meee!" they both squealed in unison. Chandler poured them both some juice and started preparing the French toast...

"Daddy?"

"Yes Kalliyah..."

"What time is everybody coming?"

"Later..."

"Okay..."

"Daddy?"

"Yes Chelsea..."

"When is Mommy having the baby?"

"Soon..." Chandler sighed...

"Daddy?"

"Yes Kalliyah..."

"We have a baby aunt right?"

"Yes Kalliyah..."

"And baby uncles – right?"

"Yes Kalliyah..."

"And all the children take a picture?"

"Yes Kalliyah..."

"Daddy?"

"Yes Kalliyah..."

"Why does Mommy have to be in the picture?"

"You don't want Mommy in the picture?"

"Mommy's not a children..."

"Yes she is!" Chelsea said... "Right Daddy?"

"Yes Chelsea..."

"But Mommy's Mommy!" Kalliyah said...

"Kalliyah – Mommy has a Mommy and Daddy – just like you…"

"Oh… so I'm gonna be a children when I grow up like Mommy?"

"Yes Kalliyah…"

"Daddy?"

"Here Kalliyah – Chelsea – eat your French toast – we need to hurry up and eat so we can get ready for everybody…" Chandler said as he placed two plates of French toast on the table and then placed a plate of French toast on the table for himself…

"Thank you Daddy!" they both said in unison as they started eating.

Chapter SIX

"Who is it?" Chandler asked as he heard knocking...

"Me..." Charles answered. Chandler got up, went to the door, looked through the keyhole...

"You got a name?" Chandler asked...

"Man – stop playin'" Charles laughed...

Aiight – hold on..." Chandler laughed as he opened the door and Charles came in...

"Uncle Charles!" the girls yelled in unison as they jumped outta their chairs and ran to him...

"Hey girls! You been good?"

"Yes!" they answered...

"Where's Mommy?"

"She's sleeping – I'll go get her..." Kalliyah said...

"No – let me go get her!" Chelsea said as she turned to run down the hall...

"Kalliyah – Chelsea – get over here – now!" Chandler boomed...

"Yes Daddy?" they both answered as they came towards him cautiously...

"When it's time for Mommy to wake up – I'll wake her up – understand?"

"Yes Daddy..." they answered...

"Good – now go in your room – and behave..."

"Okay Daddy!" they said they skipped down the hall...

"They are so cute!" Charles said...

"Thank you – Theresa sleep too?"

"Naa – she's wrapping presents and playing with Charles..."

"I'm surprised Charles is letting her wrap presents..."

"Oh that was easy – we told him his presents were at your house and Mommy needed help wrapping presents for everybody else..." Charles laughed...

"That was a good one!" Chandler laughed...

"So how'd you get the girls to behave?"

"I just told them if they want their presents they better behave..." Chandler laughed...

"I can't wait to see the look on their faces..."

"Me either..."

"Charles – come get the door!" Theresa yelled...

"Why didn't you call me? I would've helped you..." Charles said as he opened the door...

"Hi Daddy – hi Uncle Chandler – where's Kay Kay and Chelsea?" Lil' Charles asked...

"They in the room..." Chandler answered...

"Okay!" Lil Charles squealed as he ran down the hall...

"Charles!"

"Kay Kay! Chelsea!" they heard the children yell...

"Hi Theresa..." Chandler said...

"Hey Chandler – where do you want these?"

"Over there in the living room..."

"You want everything under the tree?"

"Naa – Starr's under the tree – all the other kids on the couch..."

"C'mon Theresa – I'll help you..." Charles said as he went to get up...

"Charles – sit – I got it..."

"Okay – I'll sit then..." Charles laughed...

"Naa – you can get up and help me take this food out the refrigerator!" Chandler laughed...

"Okay – whatchu got?" Charles asked as he started helping Chandler...

"We got potato salad, macaroni salad, Caesar salad..."

"Okay – watchu got for the kids?" Charles laughed...

"We got hot dogs, hamburgers, chicken nuggets, chicken wings, macaroni & cheese, pizza, and pizza bites..."

"Shit – the kids eatin' good!" Charles laughed...

"That ain't just for the kids..." Chandler laughed...

"Oh okay – what we drinkin'?"

"We got Henney..."

"You always have Henney!" Theresa laughed...

"We got Henney, Pepsi, ginger ale, Hawaiian punch, and Hi-C orange..."

"Oh Lord – these kids are gonna be high on sugar!" Theresa exclaimed...

"Oh that ain't the sugar..." Chandler laughed...

"Chandler! They don't need anything else!" Theresa laughed...

"They might not – but we do!" Chandler laughed...

"Okay!" Charles agreed...

"What else Chandler?" Theresa asked...

"We got cookies, pound cake, apple pie, cherry pie, chocolate cake, and vanilla ice cream..."

"Yea – these kids are gonna be high alright!" Theresa laughed...

"They'll be so wrapped up in their presents – they won't eat!" Charles laughed...

"Uh-uh – everybody gotta eat before we open presents!" Chandler said...

"That's right..." Starr yawned as she walked into the kitchen...

"Hey Starr – how'd you sleep?" Chandler asked as he went over to her and pulled her into a kiss...

"Uh uh – that's how you got that baby..." Charles laughed...

"That's right!" Starr laughed...

"You hungry?" Chandler asked...

"Yeesss!" Starr exclaimed...

"Sit down – I gotchu..." Chandler said as he went over to the microwave and turned it on... "You want some coffee?"

"Yea..."

"You want coffee Theresa?"

"Sure..." Theresa answered as she got up off the couch, came into the kitchen, and sat at the table with Starr...

"Here ya go..." Chandler said as he put two plates of French toast on the table...

"You made French toast! Thank you!" Starr exclaimed...

"Thank you Chandler – how'd you know I was hungry?" Theresa asked...

"Lucky guess..."

"You always wanna eat with Starr – and vice-versa!" Charles laughed...

"I do?" Theresa asked...

"Mmm hmmm..." Starr answered as she ate...

"Oh my God – Chandler – these are delicious!" Theresa exclaimed...

"Better than mine?" Charles asked...

"Honey – you don't make French toast..." Theresa answered as they all laughed...

"Hi Mommy!" Lil' Charles said as the kids came running down the hall...

"Aunt Theresa!" the girls exclaimed...

"Hi Charles, hi girls..." Theresa said as she hugged them...

"Can we open presents now?" Lil' Charles asked...

"Charles – don't start that..." Charles snapped...

"C'mon Charles – let's go behave so we can get presents..." Kalliyah said as Lil' Charles and Chelsea followed behind her and they went back in the room to play...

"Here's your coffee..." Chandler said as he placed their coffee on the table...

"Shit – we should give presents year-round..." Theresa laughed...

"We do – they get presents everyday – they get clothes, food, a roof over their head, love, family, and a room full of toys – all paid for by their parents!" Chandler laughed...

"Okay!" Charles laughed...

"Hi – I hope we're not too early..." Beautiee said as she came in the door...

"Beautiee!" Starr said as she got up and went to hug her...

"Hi Starr – take these pies..." she said...

"Sorry about that..." Starr said as she took the pies and put them on the counter...

"Hi everybody..." Beautiee said as she went to sit down on the couch...

"Beautiee – you okay?" Chandler asked...

"I'm fine... I just need... a nap..." she yawned...

"A little help guys..." Bazil said as he came in with boxes of pizza, pizza bites, and a bottle of Hennessey...

"Hi Bazil – I got it..." Charles said as he took the bottle of Hennessey from him...

"Yea Charles – that helps a lot..." Bazil laughed...

"Hi Dad – let me get those..." Chandler said as he took the boxes and put them on the island...

"Hi Daddy..." Starr said as she got up to hug him...

"Hey Starr..." Bazil said as he hugged her and kissed her on her forehead... "Hello Theresa..." he said as he held the door open...

"Uggh – this bag is heavy!" Jay said as he pulled a bag of presents in the house and Joseph followed behind him...

"Thanks for your help Jay..." Bazil said...

"You're welcome Daddy..." Jay said...

"Jay! Joseph!" Starr exclaimed...

"Starr!" they both exclaimed...

"Oh my God – you're both getting so big!"

"Baby?" Jay asked as he touched Starr's stomach...

"Baby..." Joseph said as he copied his brother...

"Hi Jay, hi Joseph..." Chandler said...

"Hi Chandler Brother..." Jay said as everyone laughed...

"Hi Chandler Brother..." Joseph repeated...

"They are so cute!" Theresa said...

"Thank you Aunt Theresa..." Jay said...

"Thank you Aunty..." Joseph said...

"No hello for me?" Charles asked as he picked up Jay and tickled him...

"Hi Uncle Charles..." Jay laughed...

"Hi Uncle..." Joseph said...

"Y'all go inside and play..." Chandler said...

"Okay!" they said as they ran down the hall and into the room...

"Jay!" "Joseph!" "Kay Kay!" "Chelsea!" "Charles!" they all yelled...

"Daddy – is Beautiee okay?" Starr asked...

"She's fine..." Bazil answered as he picked up the bag of presents and went into the living room...

"You need help with that?" Chandler asked...

"I got it..." Bazil answered as he put Starr's present under the tree and then put the rest of the presents around the living room, arranging them by color. When he was done he sat down beside Beautiee on the couch...

"Who is it?" Chandler asked...

"Troy!"

"It's open..."

"That's nice – but it would be nicer if you opened it for me..."

"Oh shoot – my bad..." Chandler said as he got up to open the door and opened it...

"Thanks for your help!" Troy said sarcastically as he came in with trays of chicken nuggets and chicken wings...

"I'm sorry – le'me help you..." Chandler said as he took the bottle of Hennessey out of Troy's hand and put it on the counter...

"Oh you real funny!" Troy snapped as he put the chicken nuggets and chicken wings on the island...

"Troy – move – this shit heavy!" Keisha said as she came in behind him with a tray of macaroni & cheese...

"Hi y'all..." Keisha said as she put the macaroni & cheese on the island behind Troy...

"Hi Troy, hi Keisha..." they all said in unison...

"Where's Amina?" Beautiee yawned...

"Hold on – Amina!" Keisha yelled as she went to open the door and stuck her head out into the hallway...

"Coming Mommy!" she beamed as she struggled to carry the bag full of presents. Keisha smiled as she watched Amina struggling with the bag. She was so proud of herself and Keisha just waited patiently...

"Mina – let Daddy..." Troy started to say be Keisha interrupted him...

"Let Daddy hold the door for you so you can bring the presents inside..."

"Okay Mommy..." she huffed... "I'm coming..."

"Thank you Amina – Mommy's big girl..." Keisha said as Amina finally made it inside with the presents. By this time all the kids came out to see what was going on and they all cheered when they saw her...

"Amina! Yaaaa!" Amina squealed with delight and started to run but Troy stopped her...

"Amina!"

"Yes Daddy?"

"You not gonna say hi?"

"Hi!" Amina said and then she ran down the hall with the kids to go play...

"Aww – she's so excited..." Theresa laughed...

"Le'me pick up these presents..." Keisha laughed as she picked up the presents and went to put them in the living room...

"Beautiee – you alright?" Keisha asked...

"Yea..." Beautiee yawned... "I'm just tired..."

"Damn girl – Bazil wearing you out like that?" Keisha laughed...

"You got jokes I see..." Bazil laughed...

"I'm not joking!" Keisha laughed...

"Hello?" Wayne asked as he opened the door and came inside holding Sky. Nobody said anything... "Am I in the wrong house?" Wayne laughed...

"Hi Dad!" Starr exclaimed when she turned around... "Is that my sister?" she asked as she went to take Sky from him and Sky started to cry...

"Sky... this is your family..." Wayne said as he comforted her...

"Family?" she asked with tears in her eyes...

"Yes Sky..."

"I don't wanna go with family..." she cried...

"You ain't gotta stay with us!" Keisha laughed...

"Hello Keisha..." Wayne laughed...

"Hi Wayne – you remember Troy?"

"Sup Wayne..." Troy said...

"You remember me Dad?" Chandler laughed...

"Hello Chandler..." Wayne laughed...

"I'm Charles – and this is my wife Theresa..." Charles said as she got up to shake Wayne's hand...

"Nice to meet you..." Wayne said...

"Hi Wayne..." Beautiee said as she got up and went to greet him...

"Hi Beautiee, Bazil – nice to see you..."

"Hello Wayne..." Bazil said without getting up...

"And who is this lil' cutie?" Beautiee asked...

"Sky..." she answered...

"Can I hold you Sky?" Sky shook her head no... "Please?" Sky looked back at Wayne...

"It's okay Sky..." Sky reached her arms out to Beautiee just as Mary walked in...

"Mommy!" Sky and Starr said in unison as Sky reached for Mary...

"You alright – hi y'all – Wayne – why didn't you hold the door open for me?"

"I'm sorry..."

"It's fine – where should I put dessert?"

"Anywhere you find room..." Chandler answered...

"Hi Bazil..."

"Hello Mary..." Bazil responded without getting up...

"Mary – I'm gonna take Sky in the other room so she can meet her brothers and her cousins..." Beautiee said...

"Wait – I'll come with you..." Mary said as she started to follow Beautiee...

"Mommy?"

"Yes Starr?"

"Where's my hug?"

"I'm sorry..." Mary laughed as she hugged her...

"I missed you!"

"I missed you too – how far along are you?"

"Five months..."

"Are you having twins again?"

"I feel like I am!" Starr laughed...

"C'mon Mary – let's go..." Beautiee said...

"I'm coming – I'm surprised Sky went to you..."

"I'm not..." Beautiee laughed...

"Still full of yourself I see..." Mary laughed...

"Of course!" Beautiee laughed as they went into the room with the kids...

"Mommy!" Jay squealed when they walked in...

"Can we open presents?" Joseph asked...

"Not yet..." Beautiee answered...

"Mommy – my sister?" Jay asked...

"Yes Jay – this is your sister – Sky..." Beautiee answered as she put Sky down...

"Oh my God – they look just like their father..." Mary whispered...

"And Sky looks just like her father..." Beautiee said...

"My sister…" Jay said as he hugged Sky. Sky was a little hesitant at first but she felt better when all the other kids came over to hug her…

"Mommy – my sister?" Joseph asked…

"Yes Joseph…" Beautiee answered…

"Beautiee – can I ask you something?"

"Sure…"

"Are you pregnant?"

"Yea…" Beautiee sighed…

"My cousin?" Amina asked…

"Yes Amina…" Beautiee answered…

"My cousin too?" Charles asked…

"Yes Charles…" Beautiee answered…

"My cousin?" Kalliyah asked…

"No Kalliyah – Sky is your Aunt…" Beautiee answered…

"My Aunt?"

"Yes…"

"My Aunt too?" Chelsea asked…

"Yes Chelsea…"

"Uncle Jay, Uncle Joseph, Aunty Sky…" Kalliyah said…

"Yes Kalliyah – you got it!" Beautiee said…

"Mommy?"

"Yes Jay?"

"Who's that?" he asked pointing at Mary…

"That's Mommy…" Sky answered…

"Hi Sky Mommy!" all the kids said in unison…

"Aww… hello…" Mary said…

"C'mon kids – let's go!" Beautiee yelled as they all ran past her towards the kitchen...

"Hey hey! Stop that runnin'!" Chandler snapped...

"But Daddy – Beautiee said let's go!" Kalliyah squealed...

"Go on then!" Chandler laughed as they all ran into the living room and jumped on Bazil...

"Good thing I wasn't trying to get a nap..." Bazil laughed...

"Mary – introduce Sky to the rest of her family..." Beautiee said...

"C'mon Sky – we'll start with your sister..." she said as she took Sky from Beautiee and handed her to Starr...

"Hi Sky..." Starr said...

"Hi Starr... my sister..." Sky said...

"This is my husband – Chandler..."

"Hi Husband Chandler..." she said as everyone laughed...

"This is Uncle Troy..."

"Hi Uncle Troy..."

"This is Aunt Keisha..."

"Hi Aunt Keisha...

This my friend Theresa..."

"Hi Theresa..."

"And this is Charles..."

"Hi Charles..."

"Now – you have one more person to meet..." Starr said as she got up and went into the living room... "This is my father..." she said as she handed Sky to Bazil...

"Beautiful Sky..." Bazil whispered as he took her and held her. Wayne watched intently as he held her... "She looks just like you Wayne..."

"She does..." Wayne agreed...

"Wayne?"

"Yes Mary?"

"Where are the presents?"

"In the car..." Wayne laughed as he went to go get them...

"Aiight – everybody in the living room..." Chandler said as they all got up to go in the living room... "We gonna do this like this: I'ma set my phone on that tripod over there – we gonna all take a picture – okay?"

"Okay!" All the kids answered in unison...

"I'm back..." Wayne said as he came in the door..."

"Okay – Wayne – put the presents down for a minute – everybody get on the couch – kids on your lap – Charles – Troy – we gonna get on the floor with the kids in front of everybody – then I'm gonna take a family photo – okay?"

"Okay!" all the kids squealed as they scrambled to their parents laps...

"Okay – hold that pose..." Chandler said as he hurried to put his phone on the tripod, set the timer, and hurry over to his spot on the floor... "Okay – smile everybody!" Chandler said.

Everyone smiled as the phone took a few pictures...

"Can we open presents now?" Chelsea asked...

"Aiight – I need all the kids on the couch!" Chandler ordered. All the kids scrambled to get up on the couch. Sky struggled but her legs wouldn't let her do it so Chandler grabbed his phone and took a quick picture as Jay reached down and pulled her up on the couch beside him...

"Aww..." everyone said in unison...

"Starr – I need you to get the bag of presents Wayne brought and give 'em out..."

"Okay Chandler..." she said as she got the bag and went to hand out the presents... "Um... Chandler?"

"Yes?"

"They don't have any names on them..."

"They're not supposed to..."

"Oh – that's right – I forgot..." she laughed as she took the first present outta the bag... "Red goes to Jay..."

"Yaaaa!" he squealed as Starr gave him his present...

"Green goes to Joseph..."

"Yaaaa!" he squealed as Starr gave him his present...

"Pink goes to Amina..."

"Yaaaa!" she squealed as Starr gave her her present...

"Silver goes to Kalliyah..."

"Yaaaa!" she squealed as Starr gave her the present...

"Gold goes to Chelsea..."

"Yaaaa!" she squealed as Starr gave her the present...

"Blue goes to Charles..."

"Yaaaa!" he squealed as Starr gave him his present...

"Purple goes to Sky..."

"Yaaaa!" she squealed as Starr gave her the present...

"And this is for me..." Starr sighed as she took out the last present wrapped in Star paper...

"Yaaaa!" all the kids said in unison...

"Okay – take your present and go sit down with the kids." Chandler waited for Starr to sit down and started taking pictures...

"Aww..." the adults all said in unison...

"Okay – now I need the grandparents to get together so I can take a picture. Wayne and Mary snuggled together immediately on the couch. Wayne was happy but when Beautiee sat next to Mary, she sucked her teeth...

"Something wrong Mary?" Wayne asked as Bazil stood beside him...

"It's nothing..." Mary sighed...

"Uh uh – y'all get up – I'on like this picture – Mary – Beautiee – y'all stand over here – Wayne – Dad – y'all stand behind 'em..." Chandler commanded. Bazil came up behind

Beautiee, pulled her to him, and held her. Wayne stood beside Bazil and smiled as he pulled Mary to him. Everyone could see how proud Wayne was...

"Aww shit — look at ch'all!" Keisha snapped...

"That's a nice picture..." Troy said...

"Look at them Babe..." Theresa said...

"I can't wait for us to be grandparents..." Charles sighed...

"Kalliyah — Chelsea — come get in the picture!"

"Okay Daddy!" they said in unison as they ran over to their grandparents...

"See — this is what I'm talkin' about!" Chandler said as he took pictures...

"I'm pregnant..." Beautiee announced...

"I fuckin' knew it!" Keisha said...

"Congratulations!" Troy said...

"God bless y'all..." Charles said...

"Amen!" Theresa agreed...

"Congratulations Daddy..." Starr said as she hugged Bazil and Chandler took the picture...

"Congratulations Beautiee..." Starr said as she hugged Beautiee and Chandler took the picture...

"Starr — come hold this phone..." Chandler said. Starr took the phone and took pictures as Chandler hugged them both...

"Baby?" Sky asked as she went over to Starr and put her hand on her stomach...

"Yes Sky – I'm having a baby..."

"Hole on – le'me get that..." Chandler said as he took the phone and took the picture...

"Okay – now I need parents and kids – Charles – you first..."

"Okay – c'mon Lil' Charles..." Charles said as Lil' Charles followed his father and mother and Chandler got the picture...

"Lil' Charles?" Mary asked...

"Yea – we call him Lil' Charles..." Theresa answered...

"Hmmm..." Mary mumbled...

"Okay – Keisha – Troy..." Chandler said...

"C'mon Amina..." Keisha said...

"I'm coming Mommy!" Amina said as she stood with her parents and Chandler got the picture...

"Okay – Wayne – Mom – Starr – Sky..." Wayne was smiling as they all got together for the picture...

"Okay – Dad – Beautiee – Starr – Jay – Joseph..." Keisha watched as Mary was seething in the corner, unaware that Keisha was aware of it, as they all got together and Chandler took the picture...

"Okay Chandler – I'll take the phone – you – Starr – Kalliyah – Chelsea..." Bazil said...

"Okay Grandpa!" They said in unison as they got together and Bazil took the picture...

"Okay – I need one more picture – Starr – Jay – Joseph – Sky…" Chandler said as Starr sat on the couch and the kids climbed up next to her…

"Sky – you sit on Starr's lap – Jay, you get on that side – Joseph - you get on that side…"

"Awww… look at them!" Keisha said…

"Okay – ready?" Chandler asked…

"Ready!" they said. The first picture was perfect – they all smiled and sat still – the next few pictures were…

"Sky – be still!" Wayne said…

"I wanna get down…" she said as she wiggled…

"Sky – wait for me…" Jay said as he reached out to take Sky's hand and Chandler got the picture…

"Cheese! Joseph said as he hugged Starr around her stomach and Chandler took the picture…

"Okay – y'all wanna eat or open presents?" Chandler asked…

"Presents!" All the kids yelled in unison as they all started jumping up and down and Chandler took that picture…

"Hold on – le'me go get this food – I'll be right back – then you can open presents – okay?"

"Yes Uncle Charles!" they all said in unison…

"C'mon Theresa – these kids are in a hurry…" Charles laughed as he took Theresa by the hand and they left to go get the hotdogs, hamburgers, chocolate cake, and ice cream. Everyone waited anxiously but they didn't have to wait long...

"Yaaaa!" they all squealed as they ran to their presents and started opening them as Chandler took pictures. Sky wasn't sure what to do so she just stood there...

"Here Sky – this is yours..." Jay said as he handed her a gift wrapped in purple paper and she tore it open...

"Jay's really sweet..." Wayne said...

"He is..." Bazil agreed.

"Troy – look at Amina!" Keisha laughed...

"I know – I see her!" Troy laughed...

"Here Sky..." Kalliyah said as she handed her a gift wrapped in purple paper and she tore it open...

"When we first got here – Sky didn't want to stay – now she probably won't want to leave..." Wayne laughed...

"I wanna stay with the family!" Sky said...

"Sure ya do – until you get older and you have to help them clean up!" Theresa laughed...

"I know – right!" Beautiee laughed...

"Here Sky..." Chelsea said as she handed her a gift wrapped in purple paper and she tore it open...

"Here Sky..." Amina said as she handed her a gift wrapped in purple paper and she tore it open...

"Here Sky..." Lil' Charles said as he handed her a gift wrapped in purple paper and she tore it open...

"Here Sky..." Joseph said as he handed her a gift wrapped in green paper...

"No Joseph – that's yours – give Sky the other one..." Bazil said. Joseph put down the gift wrapped in green paper, picked up the gift wrapped in purple paper, handed it to Sky, and she tore it open. The parents watched as the kids opened the rest of their gifts until there were two gifts left wrapped in purple paper. Sky walked over to them and picked them both up as Chandler took the picture...

"Mine?" she asked...

"Yes Sky – yours..." Mary said. Sky opened her last two gifts and Jay said... "Mommy – those are for Starr..."

"Aiight – y'all give Starr her presents!" Chandler said as he took pictures of the kids picking up the boxes and running to put the presents in Starr's lap...

"Aww – I didn't get you guys anything!"

"Daddy said the presents were for the children – and Mommy's a children – right Daddy?"

"Yes Kalliyah..." Chandler laughed...

"Starr's a children – that's cute!" Keisha said...

"Well she is!" Theresa agreed.

Chapter SEVEN

"Okay – we eatin' – then we drinkin'!" Chandler said...

"Okay!" Charles said as they all went in the kitchen...

"Y'all get in here!" Chandler yelled...

"Yes Daddy?" Kalliyah and Chelsea said in unison...

"Yes Uncle Chandler?" Amina and Charles said in unison...

"Yes Chandler Brother?" Jay and Joseph said in unison...

"Yes Chandler Husband?" Sky said as everyone laughed...

"Y'all hold hands..." Chandler said. Everyone held hands...

"Lord – we goin' make this quick..." Chandler said as all the adults laughed...

"Thank you for bringing us all together, thank you for our kids, and thank you for this food!'

"And presents!" Amina added and everyone laughed...

"Amen!" Chandler said...

"Amen!" everyone said in unison...

"Okay – kids at the table over there!" Chandler said. The kids sat at the table and all the parents made plates and set juice in front of them...

"Thank you!" they all said in unison...

"Okay – don't get up from there 'till you full..." Chandler said... "Adults in the living room!" Chandler said...

"Not you Starr – 'cause you a children..." Keisha said as they all laughed...

"Go on y'all – we got this..." Theresa said...

"Uh uh – y'all go on – we got this..." Charles said as he pulled Theresa into a kiss...

"Okay Baby..." Theresa said as she went into the living room and sat down followed by Starr, Mary, Keisha, and Beautiee...

"How long are you staying?" Beautiee asked...

"About a week..." Mary answered...

"That's nice..." Beautiee said...

"What's nice?" Bazil asked as he came into the living room with two plates followed by Chandler, Charles, Troy, and Wayne...

"They're staying for about a week..." Beautiee answered...

"That is nice..." Bazil agreed...

"The boys won't wanna leave..." Beautiee said...

"Amina won't either..." Keisha said...

"Lil' Charles acts like he lives here anyway..." Theresa laughed...

"They can stay..." Chandler said...

"I dunno Chandler... I'm tired as it is..." Starr sighed...

"Mom and Wayne will help – right?" Chandler asked...

"Well..." Mary hesitated...

"Sure..." Wayne answered...

"I'm not sure about this..." Mary said...

"It's only for tonight – let 'em hang out, eat, and play – y'all can come get your kids in the morning..." Chandler said...

"Shit – you ain't gotta beg me!" Keisha laughed...

"Okay!" Troy laughed...

"You already know..." Charles laughed...

"Beautiee?" Bazil asked...

"If they want to stay... they can stay..." Beautiee sighed...

"Good – now let's eat – then we can drink!" Chandler said...

"Mommy – we go home?" Joseph asked...

"Actually..." Beautiee sighed... "Chandler said you can stay here... if you want to..."

"I stay with Jay?"

"Yes..."

"Okay..." Joseph said with a smile...

"See?" Chandler said...

"Thank God!" Beautiee laughed...

"Why you worried?" Chandler laughed...

"Joseph NEVER wants to leave his mother..." Bazil laughed...

"He'll be alright..." Chandler said...

"Of course he will – his brother's here – and he's crazy about Amina!" Keisha laughed...

"Good thing they're not blood related – they might end up getting married one day..." Bazil laughed...

"You know what? That would really be something..." Troy said...

"I'm surprised Sky hasn't been back out here..." Wayne said...

"Give her a minute..." Mary laughed...

"She'll be alright too – she know..." Chandler said...

"Jay already claimed her too..." Charles laughed...

"You peeped that right?" Chandler laughed...

"He is sweet on her..." Bazil laughed...

"I guess we'll have to come visit more often..." Wayne said...

"Please – Sky's gonna bug the hell out of us to see them!" Mary laughed...

"Okay – I'm making drinks – Henny on deck!" Charles yelled as he got up to make drinks...

"You good to drink Mary?" Keisha asked...

"Hell yea – I got Sky off the tit as soon as she turned a year old!" Mary laughed...

"I hear that!" Keisha laughed...

"Fuck that – I was drinking while I was breastfeeding!" Theresa said...

"Really?" Mary asked...

"I sure was – I just waited until after I fed him – it's not like I was drinking every day!" Theresa laughed...

"Well... now that you mention it... Lil' Charles was a very happy baby..." Charles laughed as he came in with two glasses...

"Alright – I'ma pass 'em two at a time until we all have a glass..." Charles said as he handed two glasses to Beautiee and Mary, Keisha and Theresa, Troy and Wayne, Bazil and Chandler, and then he came back with two glasses for Starr and himself...

"I'm pregnant..." Starr said...

"I know – yours is Pepsi..." Charles said...

"To all us!" Chandler said...

"To all us!" Everyone said in unison and then they all drank...

"I love y'all..." Starr sighed...

"We love you too!" everyone said in unison...

"How's the job Wayne?" Chandler asked...

"Fine – and busy..." Wayne laughed...

"I'm surprised they let you take off..." Charles said...

"Actually – it worked out pretty easy – everyone else signed up for double-time and overtime so they didn't need me..." Wayne laughed...

"Damn!" Troy laughed...

"Oh please – they start signing up for overtime months before the holiday..." Wayne said...

"You used to work for UPS out here – right?" Bazil asked...

"Yea..."

"Did they let you carry your seniority?"

"Naa – but once they saw my resume they offered me top dollar..."

"That's wassup!" Troy said as he gave Wayne a pound...

"Well... it's about that time..." Theresa yawned...

"Damn girl – you tired already?" Keisha laughed...

"Kinda..." she yawned...

"Can't take you nowhere – you're such a lightweight..." Charles laughed...

"Charles... I'm tired..."

"I know Baby – I'm just teasing..." Charles said as he kissed her...

"Aiight then – you gonna say goodnight to your son?" Chandler asked...

"Naa..." they both said in unison as they both stood up and laughed...

"Aiight – I'ma send him over there to wake your ass up!" Chandler laughed...

"Whatever Chandler – good night y'all..." Charles said...

"Good night y'all..." Theresa yawned as they both left...

"Was it something we said?" Wayne laughed...

"Actually – it was..." Chandler answered...

"Really?" Wayne asked...

"Wayne – they're going to fuck!" Troy laughed...

"Really?" I mean – the way she was yawning... oh damn – I can't believe I fell for that!" Wayne said as everyone laughed...

"Oh my God!" Starr exclaimed...

"Starr – don't be embarrassed..." Mary said...

"After what you did to us in Toronto – nothing will ever embarrass me again!" Starr laughed...

"Oh shit – what the fuck they do Starr?" Keisha asked...

"It was nothing!" Mary said...

"Bullshit – what'd your mother do Starr?" Beautiee asked...

"Well..." Wayne started to say...

"Oh shit – now I really wanna know what y'all did!" Troy said...

"Charles and Theresa should'a stayed a little longer..." Bazil said...

"Well..." Wayne said as he got up... "I think I'll make myself another drink..." he sighed as he went into the kitchen... "As long as I'm in here – anybody else want one?"

"Just make everybody a damn drink!" Keisha laughed...

"Coming right up..." Wayne said as he took down glasses, made glasses of Hennessey on the rocks, a glass of Pepsi for Starr, and then brought the glasses in two at a time. When he finally sat down he picked up his drink, took a sip, and continued... "Well – remember – we were newlyweds – we hadn't even been married a week..."

"Okay... and?" Troy asked as he leaned in closer. Everyone sipped on their drinks as he continued...

"Well... we came up with different things to do every day... and one day we all decided to go to the beach..."

"That ain't embarrassing!" Keisha snapped...

"Well... Mary found out they had a section where clothing was optional..."

"Oooohhh!" they all said in unison...

"Y'all went to the nude beach?" Troy asked...

"We did..." Wayne answered as he smiled mischievously...

"In front of the kids?" Keisha asked...

"Hell no – I told them I'on wanna see that shit!" Chandler laughed...

"Shit – that's not embarrassing – they ain't do shit in front of you..." Keisha said...

"I know... but... I have this image of my parents... naked... on the beach... in front of strangers..."

"Shit – you get naked – don't cha?" Keisha asked...

"Of course – but I only get naked in my house!" Starr laughed...

"I don't know why you're embarrassed Starr..." Beautiee said... "It's not like they were fuckin'..."

"Oh shit!" Troy exclaimed...

"Mommy!" Starr exclaimed...

"What?" Mary laughed...

"Hmmm... sex on the beach..." Bazil said...

"Oh my God!" Starr exclaimed...

"Starr – clam down..." Chandler laughed...

"Yea Starr – calm down – it's not like this is the first time you've been embarrassed by your parents!" Beautiee laughed...

"Wai a min – what?" Chandler asked...

"Starr - you didn't tell your husband?"

"Yea... I did..."

"Tell him what dammit?" Keisha snapped...

"Starr caught us fuckin'" Beautiee said...

"Really?" Wayne asked...

"Yes Wayne – she had a key to the house – she heard us fuckin' – she came running upstairs – she thought her father was having a heart attack!' Beautiee laughed...

"I'm so sorry!" Starr exclaimed as everyone laughed...

"Starr – you don't have to apologize..." Bazil said...

"You better make sure you put a lock on your door before Sky busts in on you..." Beautiee laughed...

"I don't think we have to worry about that for a while..." Mary said...

"I didn't think so either but ever since Jay walked in on us – we didn't have a choice!" Beautiee laughed...

"My brother? He caught you?" Starr asked...

"He didn't really know what we were doing – but the next day when we got up, Jay was walking around the house saying Fuck! Fuck! Fuck!"

"Aaaaaaa Haaaaaa! Aaaaaaa Haaaaaa! Aaaaaaa Haaaaaa! Aaaaaaa Haaaaaa! Aaaaaaa Haaaaaa!" everyone laughed...

"Maybe Beautiee's right – we better put a lock on our bedroom door..." Mary laughed...

"Yo..." Troy laughed as he held his stomach..." I can't!"

"Oh my God – Chandler!"

"What Starr?"

"We have girls – and they're so nosey!"

"Aaaaaaa Haaaaaa! Aaaaaaa Haaaaaa! Aaaaaaa Haaaaaa! Aaaaaaa Haaaaaa! Aaaaaaa Haaaaaa!" everyone laughed...

"Shit – they bein' nosey ain't nothin' – I'm surprised we don't wake 'em up with all the noise we make!" Chandler laughed...

"Chandler!"

"Girl please – if nobody hears you – then he ain't hittin' it right!" Keisha laughed...

"Keisha!" Starr exclaimed...

"Shit – they ain't the only ones – you should hear them!" Chandler laughed as he pointed towards the door...

"Chandler!"

"Starr – we ain't tellin' nobody!" Keisha said...

"That's why we got a house!" Troy laughed...

"We know..." Bazil laughed...

"Fuck you mean you know?" Troy laughed...

"We hear you..." Bazil answered...

"I'on give a fuck – we hear you too!" Keisha laughed...

"Oh my God..." Mary said...

"What's wrong Mary?" Beautiee asked...

"Well..."

"What?"

"It's really quiet where we are..."

"Oh shit – the whole neighborhood done heard y'all!" Keisha laughed...

"I have a question..." Mary said...

"Okay..." Beautiee said...

"Where's the kinkiest place you've ever done it?"

"I'm not answering that..." Beautiee answered...

"That's not right Beautiee!" Mary exclaimed...

"Ewww! I don't wanna know! La la la la la..." Starr exclaimed as she covered her ears...

"Never mind..." Mary laughed...

"Well – we better get going..." Bazil said as he stood up...

"Tired eh?" Wayne asked...

"Honestly?"

"Never mind..." Wayne laughed...

"We've had a long day – and I'm a bit tired..." Bazil said...

"We gotta get going too..." Keisha said as she stood up...

"You're tired too?" Mary laughed...

"Shit – Amina wears me out – I take whatever break I can get!" Keisha laughed...

"Y'all gonna say goodnight to your kids?" Chandler asked...

"C'mon y'all – watch this..." Keisha said as she went down the hall and everyone else followed...

"Amina..."

"Yes Mommy?"

"We leavin'..."

"But I wanna stay... please?"

"You can stay – come give us a kiss..." Keisha said. Amina ran over to her parents, Troy picked her up, and she kissed her parents as they hugged her...

"You be good for Uncle Chandler and Aunty Starr – you hear me?"

"Yes Daddy – good night..." she said as she went back to playing...

"Good night y'all..." Keisha said...

"Good night y'all..." Troy said as they left...

"Jay..." Bazil said...

"Yes Daddy?" Jay answered as he came over and Joseph followed behind him...

"We're gonna leave..."

"Okay Daddy..."

"You'll be okay?"

"I'm a big boy Daddy..."

"You sure are..." Bazil said as he picked Jay up...

"Mommy – up up..." Joseph said...

"Joseph – what did Daddy tell you?"

"Mommy – pick me up please?"

"That's my good boy..." Beautiee said as she picked him up... "You be good for your sister and your big brother – understand?"

"Yes Daddy... yes Mommy..." they both said in unison. Beautiee and Bazil kissed them both, put them down, and they went back to playing...

"I hope Sky does that for us one day..." Wayne said...

"They've been around each other since they were born – Sky will get used to them too – or she'll make friends in Toronto..." Beautiee said...

"I hope so..." Mary said...

"Well – you can do one or two things..." Beautiee said...

"What's that?" Wayne asked...

"Have another baby – or make friends with a neighbor that has a baby – or both!" Beautiee answered...

"I'd like that..." Wayne said as he pulled Mary into a kiss...

"Good night y'all..." Beautiee said...

"Good night Starr..." Bazil said as he kissed her on her forehead...

"Good night Chandler – thanks for letting them stay..."

"You ain't gotta thank me Dad..." Chandler said... "Girls – say good night to your grandparents!"

"Good night!" they both said in unison...

"Good night..." Bazil laughed as he left with Beautiee...

"Mommy?"

"Yes Sky?"

"You go bye bye?" she asked with tears in her eyes...

"No Sky – we're staying here..." Wayne answered...

"Okay..." Sky said as she smiled and went back to playing...

"Chandler – I'll help you clean up while they play – Mary – Starr – go relax..." Wayne said...

"Are you sure Honey?" Mary asked...

"Mommy – Dad said go relax – let's go!" Starr laughed as she took her mother's hand and pulled her into the living room.

Chapter EIGHT

"What the hell is taking them so long?" Keisha asked...

"They can't make it too obvious..." Troy laughed...

"Here they come now..." Keisha said as Bazil and Beautiee walked outside... "Damn – it took you long enough!" Keisha snapped...

"We'll meet you at the bar..." Bazil said...

"Mary?"
"Yes Wayne?"
"Let's go to bed..."
"Now?"
"Yea – Chandler put the kids to bed..."
"Okay..."

"Good night Starr..." they both said as Mary got up and went to the guest room with Wayne...

"I hope this door has a lock on it..." Wayne whispered as he closed the door and pulled Mary into a kiss...

"I hope so too..." Wayne looked at the door, found the lock, and turned it...

"Wayne... what are you up to?" Mary whispered...

"Come with me..." he whispered as he took Mary by the hand and led her into the guest bathroom...

"Ooohhh – it's smaller than ours – but we can work with it..." Mary said as she smiled...

"We might make too much noise..." Wayne laughed...

"What can we do?"

"Well..." he answered as he went over to her and began kissing her on her neck while unbuttoning her blouse... "We can take a shower together... and..." he said before sucking on her breasts... "We can go to bed..." he said and then he kissed her... "and try to be quiet..."

"Mmmmm... I like the sound of that..."

"Here they come..." Troy said...

"Hey..." Bazil said as they all sat at a table...

"Welcome to the Martini Lounge – what can I get you?" the waitress asked...

"Four Henneys on the rocks..." Troy answered...

"Make mine a ginger ale..." Beautiee said...

"Coming right up..." the waitress said as she went to get the drinks...

"Beautiee – I peeped her on her shit – she didn't even know I was watching her..." Keisha said...

"Oh I know!" Beautiee laughed...

"What'd I miss?" Troy asked...

"She was cool until Chandler said he wanted a picture with the grandparents..." Keisha answered...

"What'd she do?" Troy asked...

"Here's your drinks..." the waitress said as she put them down on the table...

"Thank you..." Bazil said as Keisha continued...

"She was in the corner – mad as hell!" Keisha laughed...

"I saw that..." Bazil agreed...

"Ain't shit changed..." Keisha said...

"So – we went down the hall with Sky to introduce her to the kids – she gonna say oh I'm surprised Sky went to you – and I said I'm not – so she gonna say – still full of yourself I see..."

"Wow..." Troy said...

"What'd you say?" Bazil asked...

"I told her I sure am!" Beautiee laughed...

"I hear that!" Keisha laughed as they high-fived...

"You did good tonight..." Beautiee said as she pulled Bazil into a kiss...

"I do good every night..." Bazil said...

"I know that's right!" Troy laughed as they gave each other a pound...

"I know it was hard for you to sit there with Wayne..." Beautiee said...

"Beautiee..." Bazil breathed as he kissed her... "Wayne isn't a threat to me – he never was – he never will be..."

"Okay!" Troy exclaimed...

"Wayne was on pins and needles..." Bazil said...

"He was..." Troy agreed...

"How you know Troy?" Keisha asked...

"Trust me – I know..."

"He's happy..." Beautiee said...

"I could see that..." Keisha said...

"He should be..." Bazil said...

"Why you say that?" Keisha asked...

"He has the wife he always wanted, the life he always wanted, and the child he always wanted..." Bazil answered...

"Sky is his daughter?" Keisha asked...

"Keisha – you don't need a DNA test to know that – Sky looks just like him!" Troy exclaimed...

"He'll stay happy... and long as Mary doesn't hurt him..." Bazil said...

"Oh shit – you think Mary will hurt him?" Troy asked...

"I hope not – for her sake..." Bazil answered...

"Damn Bazil – why you say that?"

"Because..." Bazil said as they finished their drinks... "if she hurts him again... he'll kill her..." Bazil said as he took Beautiee by the hand and helped her up...

"Good night..." Beautiee said...

"Good night..." they both said in unison...

"Good night..." Bazil said as they left the bar and went to their hotel room...

"Damn – you think Wayne would kill Mary?" Keisha asked...

"Hell yea!" Troy answered...

"Why you say that?"

"Think about it Keisha – she put that man through a lot – and she was fuckin' Bazil while she was with him!"

"Oh shit – I forgot about that – you right..."

"Let's go..."

"Okay..." Keisha said as they got up from the table and left the bar...

"Beautiee..." Bazil breathed as he kissed her eyes and then her mouth... "What's wrong?"

"I'm sorry..." she whispered as tears came down her face...

"You have nothing to be sorry for..." he said as he pulled her into a kiss and held her...

"I can't help it – I keep going back to the last time we were here..."

"Yes..." he said as he began kissing her neck and started undressing her...

"You brought me my favorite outfit..." she breathed...

"Yes..." he breathed as he slid her pants and panties off her...

"I was so happy..."

"So was I..." he breathed in her ear as he pulled her close to him and ran his hands up her back...

"I love you..."

"I love you too..." he said as he pushed her back down onto the bed and took of his clothes...

"Ooohhh... is that for me?" she asked as she looked at his erection...

"You want it?" Bazil asked...

"Yes..." Beautiee breathed...

"Tell me..." Bazil said as he walked over to the bed, stroking his dick...

"I want it..." Beautiee breathed...

"Tell me what you want..." Bazil breathed as he spread her legs, climbed on top of her, eased himself inside her... and Beautiee started laughing...

"Am I tickling you?" he asked...

"No..." she laughed...

"Okay... what's so funny?"

"You said tell you what I want... and..." she laughed...

"Beautiee..." he laughed... "What's so funny?"

"I want what Jay said!" she laughed...

"Oooohhh – you wanna Fuck! Fuck! Fuck!" Bazil laughed...

"Yes – I wanna Fuck! Fuck! Fuck!" Beautiee laughed...

"So do I..." Bazil breathed as he started thrusting and Beautiee locked her feet behind his back...

"I can't wait to go to bed..." Keisha said as she closed the door...

"Okay!" Troy exclaimed...

"Troy?"

"Yes Keisha?"

"This is our first night alone since we've had Amina..." she said as she pulled him into a kiss...

"I know..."

"We can make all the noise we want..." she said as they continued kissing...

"I know..." Troy said as they continued kissing...

"Wait a minute..." Keisha said as she went to get a chair and sat in it...

"Keisha – whatchu doin'?"

"Dance for me..." she said as she turned on the music...

"Okay! Okay!" Troy said as he started dancing and doing a strip tease for Keisha...

"Yea... just like that baby... I like that shit..." she said as Troy continued dancing and stripping until he was completely naked. Troy walked over to Keisha with his belt in his hand...

"Troy..."

"Stand up..." he commanded...

"Okay..." Keisha said as she stood up and Troy put the belt around her...

"Come here..." he said as he led her to the bed, walking backwards, fell back on the bed, and pulled Keisha down on top of him...

"Wayne..." Mary whispered...

"Yes Mommy..." he breathed...

"I'm cumming..."

"I'm cumming with you..." Wayne breathed as he started fucking her harder and deeper...

"Wayne... that's it... right there... yes... fuck me!"

"Uggh! Uggh! Uggh! Uggh! Uuuugggghhhh!"

"So much for being quiet..." Mary laughed...

"Chandler..." Starr moaned...

"Ssshhh..." Chandler whispered...

"I can't help it..." Starr moaned. Chandler kissed her, put his tongue in her mouth, and covered her mouth with his to muffle her sounds… "Mmmm….. Mmmm….. Mmmm….. Mmmm….. Mmmmmmmmmmm!"

Mmmph! Mmmph! Mmmph! Mmmph! Mmmmpppphhhh!"

"Lil' Charles should stay over there more often…" Theresa breathed…

"I think so too…" Charles breathed…

"Ever since I had him…" she breathed… "I can't get enough dick!"

"I know…"

"Charles… Charles… Charles…"

"You're so fuckin' wet!" Charles breathed as he spread her legs wider and fucked her deeper…

"Charles! Oh God! Fuck me! I'm cumming!"

"Uggh! Uggh! Uggh! Uggh! Uuuugggghhhh!"

"That was so fucking good!" Theresa breathed as she pulled Charles into a kiss…

"Mmmm…" Charles breathed… "I like what's gotten into you…"

"That would be you…" Theresa breathed as they continued kissing.

"Mommy?" Sky yawned…

"Hi Sky…" Jay yawned…

"Where's Mommy?"

"She's sleeping…"

"Mommy's sleeping?"

"Uh uh…"

"I want Mommy…" Sky said as she jumped up…

"Sky… No…" Jay said…

"But I want Mommy…" she said as she started to tear up…

"Don't cry Sky…" Jay said as he got up and hugged her…

"Okay…" she sniffed…

"Hi…" Joseph said as he yawned…

"Hi Joseph…" Jay said…

"Hi…" Amina yawned…

"Hi!" Chelsea and Kalliyah said in unison...

"Hi!" Sky beamed...

"Hi..." Charles yawned...

"I want Mommy..." Sky said...

"Let's play while Mommy and Daddy are sleeping..." Kalliyah said...

"But I'm hungry..." Chelsea whined...

"I'll be right back..." Kalliyah said as she opened the door and tip-toed down the hall to the kitchen. When she got to the kitchen, she climbed up in the chair and picked up the box of cookies just as Chandler walked into the kitchen...

"What are you doin'!" Chandler yelled. Kalliyah started to cry and Chandler felt bad... "C'mere Kalliyah – it's okay..." he said as he hugged her...

"I'm sorry... Chelsea's... hungry... Mommy's sleeping..." she sniffed...

"Look – I'ma let you take these cookies – but I need you to do something for me..."

"Okay Daddy..."

"I need y'all to stay quiet so Mommy can sleep okay?"

"Okay Daddy!" Kalliyah yelled as she ran down the hall with the cookies. Chandler laughed and shook his head as he heard Kalliyah loud and clear... "Daddy said we can have cookies!"

"Yaaaa!" they all yelled in unison...

"You gave them cookies?" Wayne asked as he came into the kitchen...

"I caught Kalliyah tryin' to sneak and take them so... yea..." Chandler laughed...

"You have coffee?"

"I was just getting' ready to make a pot..."

"Perfect..." Wayne sighed...

"I'on know if my coffee's perfect – but I'll make some..." Chandler laughed as he got up, went to get the coffee out of the cabinet, and started making coffee...

"Good morning..." Mary yawned as she came into the kitchen...

"How'd you sleep?" Chandler asked...

"Wonderfully..." Mary sighed...

"So did I..."Wayne sighed as he pulled Mary into a kiss...

"Good morning..." Starr yawned as she came into the kitchen...

"Good morning Starr – how'd you sleep?" Mary asked...

"I'm fine..." Starr sighed. Wayne and Mary looked at each other and smiled... "Where are the girls?" Starr asked as she sat down...

"They in there eatin' cookies..." Chandler answered...

"Chandler! Why would you do that?"

"You hear that?"

"What? I don't hear anything..."

"Exactly..." Wayne laughed...

"Somebody's at the door — I'll get it..." Starr said as she got up to answer the door...

"Good morning — where's Charles?" Charles asked as he came into the kitchen...

"Good morning..." Theresa said as she came in behind Charles...

"Good morning y'all — he's in the room with the rest of 'em..." Chandler answered...

"Let me go see my son..." Charles said as he started to go down the hall...

"Charles!' Theresa exclaimed...

"What?"

"Leave 'im be!" she laughed...

"Alright, alright!" he laughed...

"How'd y'all sleep?" Chandler asked. They didn't answer — they both bust out laughing... "We slept great..." Chandler laughed...

"Someone's at the door — you want me to get it?" Charles asked...

"Sure..." Chandler said...

"Good morning — c'mon in!" Charles exclaimed as he opened the door for Bazil, Beautiee, Troy, and Keisha...

"Ooohhh... I smell coffee..." Beautiee said as she sat down...

"Good morning Beautiee, good morning Daddy..." Starr said...

"Good morning everybody..." Beautiee yawned...

"Good morning everybody..." Bazil said...

"Good morning y'all…" Keisha said as she made her way into the kitchen…

"Morning…" Troy said as he came in behind her…

"Okay – coffee's done – I'm making two cups – one for me – one for Starr – everybody else on their own…" Chandler said…

"That's fine…" Wayne said…

"I'm making breakfast…" Bazil said…

"That's okay Dad – I got it – I just need to have a cup of coffee first…" Chandler said…

"Son?" Bazil asked…

"Yes Dad?"

"I'm making breakfast…"

"Yes Dad…" Chandler laughed…

"Need any help?" Wayne asked…

"I'm good – thanks for asking…"

"Mind if I watch?"

"Actually – I'd rather you didn't…"

"No offense…"

"None taken…"

"I'm gonna feed the kids first…"

"Okay – Sky's a little fussy though – don't take it personal if she doesn't eat…" Wayne said

"She's been eating cookies – she probably won't be hungry…" Mary said…

"I'm gonna get us some coffee…" Charles said as he got up, went over to the counter, and made two cups of coffee…

"Thanks Babe…" Theresa said…

"I need everyone to go in the living room – I need the kitchen..." Bazil said...

"Damn shame I'm getting' kicked outta my kitchen..." Chandler laughed as he got up...

"I'm sorry Chandler – would you rather I not cook?"

"Oh no – I'ma be right in the living room – c'mon Starr..." Chandler said as he took Starr by the hand and led her into the living room with their coffee...

"Wait a minute – you're gonna make me spill my coffee..." she laughed...

"We're right behind you..." Charles laughed...

"Troy – can you bring my coffee in the living room?" Keisha asked...

"Yea..."

"Okay – thank you – I love you..."

"I love you too..." Troy said as he was making their coffee. When he was done he took both cups of coffee into the living room and sat down beside Keisha...

"I'll get us some coffee..." Wayne said as he got up and went over to the counter. Bazil watched him intently as he made coffee for Mary and himself... "Am I in your way?"

"Not at all – take your time..."

"I'm done – c'mon Mary – let's go in the living room..." he said as he carried both cups of coffee and Mary got up and followed him into the living room...

"I'll be right with you..." Bazil said as he went over to Beautiee and kissed her...

"Mmmm... okay..." she sighed. Bazil took two more cups out of the cabinet, put them on the counter, and made coffee...

"Here..." Bazil said as he handed Beautiee the coffee...

"Mmmm... this is delicious – thank you..."

"You're welcome..."

"Ummm... Beautiee?" Keisha asked...

"I'm coming..." she laughed as she went into the living room...

"Mommy?" Sky said as she came into the kitchen with a cookie in her hand...

"Good morning cutie..." Bazil said...

"I want Mommy..."

"She's in the living room..."

"Mommy!" Sky yelled as she ran to Mary..."

"How's my big girl?" Mary asked..."

"I'm fine..."

"Sky... come see Daddy..." Wayne said...

"Okay..." she beamed as she threw herself into his arms...

"I love you..." Wayne said as he kissed her on her forehead...

"I love you Daddy – bye!" she said as she ran back in the room with the kids...

"She's cute – she acts just like Amina..." Keisha said...

"Long as they can see your face – they aiight..." Troy said...

"Smells good..." Wayne said...

"It will be..." Bazil said...

"I guess I'm finally getting the meal we were promised..." Charles laughed...

"Naa... we still owe you..." Chandler said...

"Fine with me!" Theresa laughed. Bazil took the pancake batter down from the cabinet, opened it, poured in in a mixing bowl, added some chocolate chips to the mix, and proceeded to make mini pancakes...

"Hi Daddy!" Jay said as he came into the kitchen...

"Hello Jay..." Bazil answered as he continued making pancakes...

"Daddy's cooking..."

"Yes Jay... Daddy's cooking..."

"Hi Mommy – Daddy's cooking..." Jay said as he went into the living room...

"Hi Jay..." Beautiee said...

"Hi..." Jay said as he waived to everybody...

"Hi Jay..." everyone said in unison...

"Daddy?" Joseph said as he came into the kitchen...

"Yes Joseph?"

"I go with Jay?"

"He's in the living room..."

"Hi Mommy..." Joseph said as he walked into the living room...

"Hi Joseph..." Beautiee said... "Say hello to everybody..."

"Hi everybody..."

"Hi Joseph..." everyone said in unison...

"C'mon Joseph..." Jay said as he took Joseph by the hand and they went back in the room...

"They're really cute..." Wayne said...

"Thank you..." Beautiee said...

"Breakfast is ready!" Bazil said...

"Yaaaa!" the kids yelled in unison as they all ran into the kitchen and sat at the table...

"Here ya go!" Bazil said as he put three plates of mini chocolate-chip pancakes on the table...

"Pancakes!" Amina said...

"I don't want pancakes..." Sky said...

"Here Sky..." Jay said as he picked one up and handed it to her...

"Uh uh..." Sky said as she shook her head back and forth...

"It's good Sky..." Jay said as he took a bite and then handed it back to her. Sky took a bite and chewed it...

"Mmmm..." she said...

"Oh shit – she's eating pancakes..." Wayne laughed...

"Jay has a way with her..." Mary said...

"Look at Amina..." Keisha said...

"Look at Charles!" Theresa said...

"I still can't believe Sky's eating pancakes..." Wayne laughed...

"Make 'em small – add chocolate chips... done!" Bazil said...

"Ohhh – no wonder they're eating pancakes!" Mary laughed...

"Daddy always makes that when he comes over..." Starr said...

"Oh – so now we're gonna hear pancakes, pancakes, pancakes!" Mary laughed...

"Who's ready for juice?" Bazil asked...

"Me!" they all answered in unison...

"Me!" Sky repeated...

"Coming right up..." Bazil said as he went over to the cabinet, took down cups, got the juice out of the refrigerator, poured the juice, and put the cups on the table...

"Thank you Daddy..." Jay and Joseph said...

"Thank you Grandpa..." Kalliyah and Chelsea said...

"Thank you Uncle Bazil..." Charles and Amina said...

"Mommy?" Sky said...

"Yes Sky?"

"Who's that?" she asked, pointing at Bazil...

"That's my father..." Starr answered...

"Thank you my father..." Sky said...

"Aww... she's too cute!" Theresa said...

"She'll get it – she hasn't been around them but a minute..." Keisha said...

"All done?" Bazil asked...

"Yes Daddy!" Jay answered...

"What do we do when we're all done?"

"We clean up Daddy...' Jay said as he picked up his plate, his cup, and put them in the garbage. Wayne and Mary watched as Kalliyah, Chelsea, Amina, Charles, and Joseph cleaned up behind themselves...

"Me too..." Sky said as she cleaned up behind herself...

"She's something else..." Beautiee said...

"Thank you Beautiee..." Mary said...

"Okay – now I can get down to business..." Bazil said as he started preparing breakfast for the adults. Bazil started by taking the bacon, onions, peppers, cheese, eggs, potatoes, and biscuits out the refrigerator. After he turned the oven on to pre-heat, he lit the flame under the frying pan and dropped the bacon in...

"I can't wait for this..." Charles said. Bazil washed the potatoes, chopped them up into cube-size, put them on a baking pan, seasoned them, and put them in the oven along with the biscuits. The bacon was done so Bazil put the bacon on a plate of paper towels to absorb the grease and chopped up the onions and peppers, and put them in the pan in olive oil. While the onions and papers were cooking, he scrambled one dozen eggs, added a cup of cream, beat it some more, and put it to the side. After he chopped up the bacon, he added it to the pan, poured in the scrambled eggs, cooked it until it was just about done, and then added cheddar cheese...

"Damn that smells good!" Charles said...

"It is..." Bazil said as he took the potatoes and biscuits out the oven, turned the oven off, took down the plates, prepared them, and set the table... "Breakfast is ready..." Bazil said as everyone came into the kitchen...

"Oh wow! This looks good!" Charles said...

"It is!" Troy said as everyone sat down...

"Thank you Daddy..." Starr said...

"You're welcome..."

"Thank you Daddy..." Chandler said...

"You're welcome Chandler..."

"Thank you Bazil..." Charles said...

"Everybody's welcome —let's eat – I wanna hear what Charles has to say..."

"Huh? Oh – it's good!" Charles said...

"It's good..." Theresa said...

"It's delicious..." Wayne said...

"It's really good..." Mary said...

"Thank you..." Bazil said...

"Told y'all..." Troy said as he ate...

"Mmm hmm..." Keisha agreed...

"I love when Daddy cooks..." Starr said...

"Me too..." Chandler agreed...

"Well..." Bazil said as he finished his food... "That was delicious..." he said as he got up from the table, went over to the cabinet, took down the coffee, and made a fresh pot.

Twisted Christmas
The Next Generation Tree

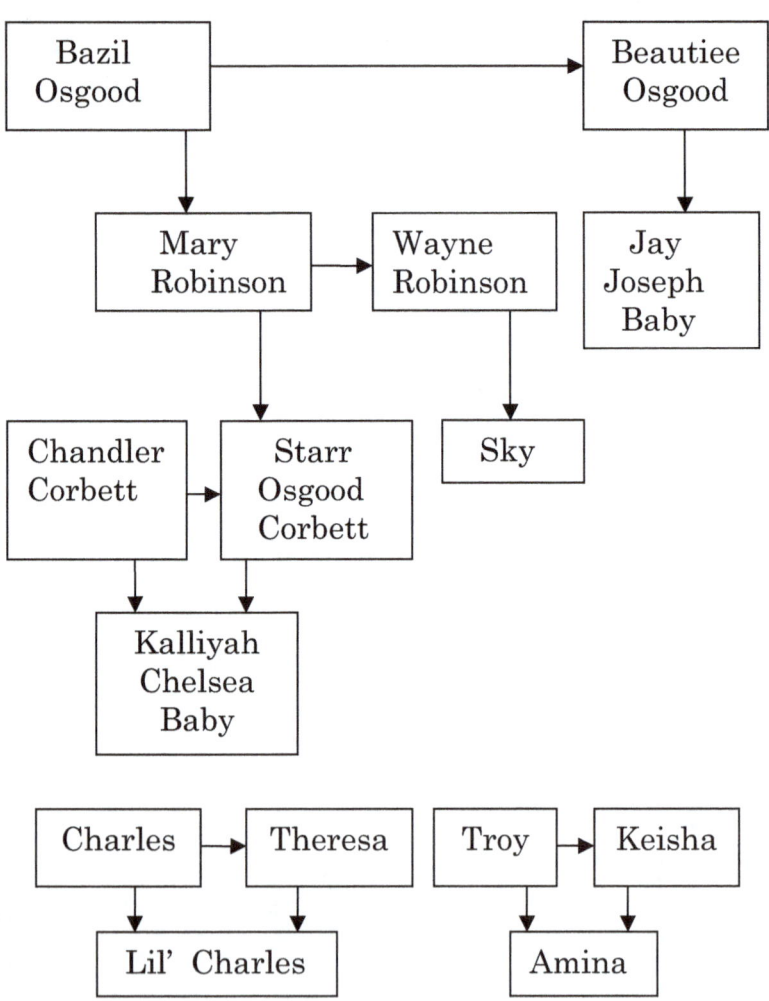

Twisted Christmas
The Next Generation Tree

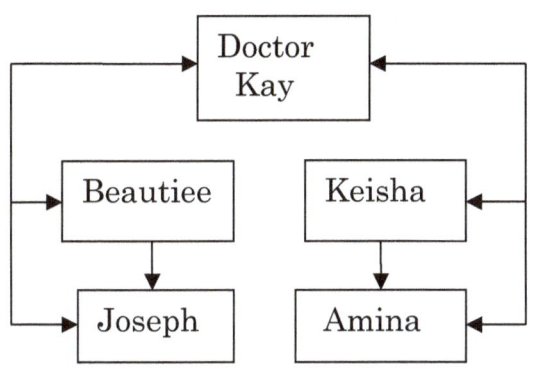

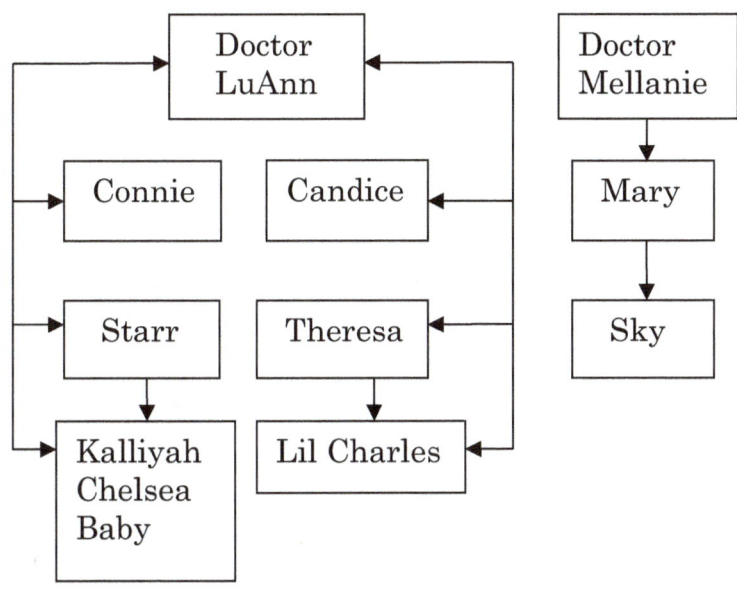